The Serendipity of Flightless Things

Fiadhnait Moser

 YELLOW JACKET

For Aunt El and Uncle Chaz

※ **YELLOW JACKET**

An imprint of Little Bee Books

251 Park Avenue South, New York, NY 10010

Text copyright © 2019 by Rachel Moser-Hardy

All rights reserved, including the right of reproduction in whole or in part in any form.

Yellow Jacket and associated colophon are trademarks of Little Bee Books.

Interior design by Veronique Lefevre Sweet

Manufactured in the United States of America LAK 0719

First Edition

10 9 8 7 6 5 4 3 2 1

Library of Congress Cataloging-in-Publication Data is available upon request.

ISBN 978-1-4998-0843-8

yellowjacketreads.com

Pronunciation Key

NAMES

Aobh (EEV)

Aoife (EE-fa)

Ciara (KEE-rah)

Conn (KON)

Ena (EN-ya)

Fiachra (FEE-a-khra)

Fiadhnait (FEE-ah-nawt)

Finnuala O'Dálaigh-Sé (fin-OO-lah oh-DAWL-ee SHAY)

Lir (LEER)

Lorcan (LOR-can)

Nuala (NOO-la)

bodhrán (BOW-ran) — an Irish frame drum with a goatskin (or other animal skin) head tacked to one side with the other side open-ended in order to control the pitch and timbre

craic (crack) — a term for news, gossip, fun, entertainment, and enjoyable conversation

lough (lock) — a lake or partially landlocked or protected bay

PART I

Ireland

Chapter 1

August 1971

MY THREE BEST FRIENDS lived inside a silver locket. Their names were Oliver, Ed, and Margaret, and all three were dead. That locket was one of the four things I brought with me to America—the locket, my Sunday dress, my orphanage of hawthorn leaves, and the nine hundred stories my grandmother gave me. The day Grandma Nuala passed the locket on to me, I should have died. And it all began with a particular isle, a bird pale as seafoam, and a sprig of heather far luckier than me.

Nuala gripped my hand as if she were walking me to grade school for the first time—tight, cold, brave. The way you'd hold a prayer bead. Her knees quivered as we took our final step to the tip-top of the Slieve League Cliffs and I pulled her over a moss-spotted boulder. When at last we reached the overlook, Nuala bent down, taking me with her. We sat a finger's width from death, feet dangling off the ledge. Her fingers slipped from mine as my body went limp with awe.

"There it is." The wind carried away my words, lilting a banshee song so sad and sweet and aching with all the longing of a thousand stories. "Inis Eala."

"Aye, lass," breathed Nuala. It was the sort of breath she usually spent on dandelion clocks or eyelash wishes. "Best view in all of Ireland." She stretched out a wrinkled, dirt-caked hand toward the isle as if trying to touch it. "You know, even when the greyman's out and about with his bucket of fog, spooking even the finest sailors, you can still see that isle from here." She kissed the top of my head and whispered, "Happy birthday, Finn."

The isle rose like a lighthouse on the horizon, tall and emerald striped. My North Star, it guided me when I was lost; my Neverland, it listened to me when I was alone, which happened to be rather often. Nuala said that was because I had a "refined" taste in friends. My teacher, Mrs. Flanagan, said it was because most children don't take their four o'clock tea and biscuits with an island for company.

Though not once had I set foot on the isle, I knew its every inch like I knew my own home. Inis Eala and I had had hundreds of conversations—in rain, in snow, even once in a hailstorm. I had it memorized, from its lone dust mite of a ramshackle cottage to its speck of a white-flowered hawthorn tree hanging off the westernmost edge. Today, the hawthorn dripped scarlet berries, blooming like pinpricks of blood on a lace napkin.

Nuala plucked a sprig of heather and let it flutter in her pinch, and I pulled loose a scarlet ribbon from my wrist. "They say it's the home of the swan children," I said, as I played tug-of-war with the wind—my hair, the rope.

"Indeed they do," said Nuala. Her hand landed on my scalp, and she took the ribbon and wrangled my hair into a ponytail, tucking the heather behind my ear.

A dewdrop slipped off the stem and down my earlobe, like a child down a slide. When I was small and scared of night howls, Nuala would take me out to the wildflower garden and tell me about the dew and the heather. "Don't you see their tears?" she would say. "Can't you hear the heather's lament? They're sisters with the sun, see, and when she sails off to America at dusk, the heather weeps. That's what goes a-wailin' in the nighttime, Finn. Just a field of souls as mournful as our own." And then I could sleep.

I waited for Nuala to say more, but she didn't, so I cast my eyes down to the blissfully swaying sea. And then slowly, carefully, I ventured, "So . . . what d'you think? Can I go?" I spared a glance up to Nuala and spat out, "I'm twelve now, plenty old 'nough. *Please?*"

A perpetual hurricane whirred behind Nuala's eyes. I feared her—most everyone did—but loved her too, most days more than I feared her. "No."

Something in my chest plummeted. "But it can't be so dangerous. Da says that Ma used to visit all—"

"You know nothing of that. Do not speak of things you do not understand." Nuala squeezed shut her eyes as if my words had chopped a sliver off her shoulder. When she opened her eyes, she added in gentler tones, "Just don't talk about her."

"Sorry," I mumbled. "It's just—I've got it all planned out, I've learned to swim, everythin'. I've been charting swans for months—*years* practically—and collecting stories from the village folk and the trees and the Ogham runes. I just . . . *have* to see them."

Nuala said nothing. I took the sprig of heather from behind my ear and began to tear off the pink-purple blossoms, letting them fly away to Inis Eala. How unfair it was that such tiny things could simply flutter off to wherever they pleased, whenever they pleased. I was a thousand times bigger, yet still I was stuck in Donegal, and the blossoms caught free flights to my dream. I closed my eyes, breathed. "I've never wanted anythin' more in all my life."

Nuala stood, took my hand, and pulled me up. She pursed her lips and said, "My answer is no, Finn. That's my final w—"

"But you want to see 'em too, don't you? I can see it in your own two eyes, the way you look at—"

"Finnuala O'Dálaigh-Sé." My mouth snapped shut. Even the wind grew quiet and the heather stood still. "I only say it for your—"

"Protection, I know." My shoulders sagged, and I turned from Nuala, a hollow feeling creeping under my skin.

At those words, something sounded below—a low, steady *thrump-ah-thrump-ah-thrump-ah-thrump*. Like the sea had grown a heartbeat. I spared a glance down into the abyss to see if I could spot a selkie, seal skin covering their maiden form, perhaps cloud-watching on a rock, but there was just water.

I took a gulp of sea-salt air and stuffed my hands into my pockets. "So, when *can* I go? When will I be old 'nough, strong 'nough?"

"You may go when you are needed there."

I bit my lip. "*So never.*"

"I'm not fond of that word. *Never,*" spat Nuala. Her lips puckered and nose crinkled as if the word had left a tarry taste in her mouth. "Not fond at all."

"Sorry," I said, tracing a circle in the dirt with the toe of my sneaker. "I just . . . I know they don't need me, but I need *them*. I need the swans. I need Inis Eala, and I need the story."

"And you'll have the story," said Nuala, taking my hand.

I kicked a speckling of dirt over my circle and looked up to her. "In time," she whispered, "when I have gone, the story will be yours."

"Gone?" I choked on the word. A feeling of vertigo took hold of my knees and I stumbled back with a particularly strong gust of wind. A colony of dried oak leaves rattled through the grass and off the cliff's edge. "Wh- what do you mean?"

I gripped Nuala's hand tighter. For some reason, her fingers felt frailer, each wrinkle now a scar I wanted to heal instead of a story I wanted to hear. "You'll always be around," I said. "Always. Won't you, Nuala?"

Nuala let go of my hand and reached up to the nape of her neck. There was a tiny tinkle of metal clinking, and Nuala revealed a tarnished silver necklace.

"Your locket?"

Nuala nodded. "*Your* locket, now," and she enclosed it in my palm. "This way, you'll always have me around. You'll never be alone."

And as if it held all the stories I'd ever been told, I gently opened the latch. Inside was a black-and-white photograph of three children sitting on a tree branch: one girl, head tossed back in laughter; and two boys, one wearing an impish grin and the other smiling shyly away from the camera.

"Who are they?" I asked, hooking the locket around my neck. "The children."

Nuala half opened her mouth to speak, but as she did, the thumping returned, stronger now. And this time, I had the uncanny feeling that someone was listening to us. But that didn't make any sense, all the way up here.

Worry lines laced Nuala's eyes as I whispered, "Did you hear—"

I ducked as something cold, fast, and *feathery* swooped up from below the cliff and over my head; my foot caught the edge of the cliff, and I toppled back. My scarlet ribbon spiraled into the blue below, the breeze cushioning its fall like it would a parachute. The purple and gray of the sky swirled together in a dour bruise, and white feathers caught on my eyelashes like snowflakes, just as cold.

"Finn!" The beating of the bird's wings muffled Nuala's voice so to sound as if she were shouting my name all the way from Inis Eala.

I grappled for dandelion sprouts, clawed at the just-rained-on dirt turning to mud beneath my fingernails—and then I was falling. "NUALA!" My stomach lurched as if I were stuck on a merry-go-round, and as I sped downward, the world slowed in my eyes. Nuala's face was ashen, her fingers still outstretched over the cliff's ledge even though I must have been a dozen feet below her reach. There was something about the veins in her fingers I hadn't noticed before—they shone vivid blue through translucent skin, like veins of a cornflower corpse preserved in pages of a hundred-year-old book. They mirrored in her forehead, around her eyes, under her collarbone—

Something was choking me. I gagged, and my hands lunged for my throat—the locket was clenched tight around my neck, strangling me.

I yanked to pull it free, before it occurred to me that either way—by strangulation or free-falling impact from the cliff—I was going to die.

But if that was so, why was I going up, not down?

Gravity turned itself on end, and I peeked up and glimpsed two muddy, bat-wing-like *feet*! They clutched the silver chain of my locket still cutting into my throat, and a pair of wide, pale wings flapped heavily against the wind. I counted the wings' beats—*one, two, three*—and then remembered that was a trick for falling asleep, not staying alive.

The ground caught me by surprise. I tumbled head-first into a thistle patch, spat prickles from my mouth, and wiped grime from my cheeks with grimier hands. And then arms enveloped me in a rosemary-soap-and-burnt-brambleberry-pie-smelling hug. I nestled my head in Nuala's patchwork sweater as she lilted over and over, *"My Finnuala, my Finnuala, my Finnuala . . ."*

Nuala huffed and leaned back, examining me from arm's length as if I were a puzzling abstract statue in a museum. She then patted my cheeks, pinched some warmth back into them, and heaved, "Don't you ever scare me like that again, Finn, don't you *dare.*"

But I wasn't in the mood for making promises. I squinted past Nuala's shoulder; the bruised sky had flushed a sickly mauve, and I searched for a scab of white somewhere in the horizon. "Where'd it go?"

Nuala narrowed her eyes. "Where'd what go?" I stood and whirled twice around, Nuala leaping to catch hold of my wrist. "What in heaven's n—"

"You know, the bird—a swan, I think," I said, my heart trilling against my rib cage. "It saved me. And—" My hand lunged to my neck, but was greeted only by an even more pronounced hollowness than I had felt before. "The locket—it's gone."

Nuala's mouth twitched, but she plastered on a smile and stuttered, "D-don't fret, it's just a silly piece of jewelr—"

"That's what it wanted, en't it? It came for me and my locket. And then . . ." I looked around. The water below had stilled, and not even a distant big-bellied *honk* or the slightest ruffling of feathers could be heard. "It disappeared."

"Haven't a clue what you're talking about," said Nuala, shaking her head in concern. "You took a tumble backward, but caught hold of the cliff, and thank our lucky stars you did."

I gaped at her. "You're telling me you *never* saw it—the bird, massive and white and strong as an archer's bow?"

"It was a blackbird, lass," soothed Nuala. "Certainly not a swan. But it did nothing more than give you a fright." She bit her lip and laid a hand on my forehead. "Feel a tad warm, perhaps you've—"

I shook Nuala's hand away. "I know what I saw."

Nuala smiled pitifully at me and pulled me up by the elbow. "You're in shock, lass; let's go home. We'll bake a birthday pie, whatever kind you like."

My mind was about as far from pies as it was from promises. "No," I breathed, an idea creeping into my head. "Er—no thanks, I've got to go to the willows."

"Finn, you just *fell off a cliff*—"

"You always say it, don't you? Never break a date with a willow."

The willows were the most magical grove of trees in all of Donegal. Secrets whispered among their leaves, a place where the dead and the living could hold hands if even for but a moment.

The willows would help; they would always help. Stories rumbled through their veins, cracked down their branches like the spines of old books. I simply had to find that swan. It had come for me. I could feel it in my bones.

Nuala sighed. "Best not be late. You don't want to end up on a willow's bad side. Would you like my company?"

"I—I think I'll go alone, thanks."

Nuala nodded. "See you for supper, then. But, Finn?"

"Yeah?"

"I don't want you going near Inis Eala," she said sternly. "One day, perhaps, but not now. Not yet. It is a faery place, and faery do not take kindly to uninvited visitors. Try to swim, and the waters will be restless. Try to row, and they will be twice so. Fly a plane there, and in one breath, they'll blow you all the way to Madagascar. Do you understand me?"

I nodded. "Sure, Nuala."

"No 'Sure, Nuala' today. You've got to *promise*." Sometimes I had the oddest feeling Nuala could gaze straight through me, as if my mind were a looking glass to her.

My fingers fiddled with a hole in my sweater, stretching it twice as big. Never had I broken a promise with Nuala before, and I didn't intend to start now. When at last I spoke, my voice chipped on the words. "I promise."

Nuala nodded delicately. "Pick up some blackberries from Mrs. McLean in the village when you're through, why don't you?" she said. "We're runnin' a touch low."

I nodded and scampered down the Slieve League Cliffs, quick as my feet would carry me. Nuala was right—it was best to keep on a willow's good side.

Chapter 2

WHEN I CAME TO THE WILLOW GLADES, a small place tucked between two hills, all I wanted to do was tell Grandpa Oliver about the swan and Inis Eala and how I wouldn't be traveling there like I'd been planning for practically ever. Also about Nuala, how transparent her skin had seemed, how blue her veins had looked, how wrinkly her hands had felt. How fragile.

I found Oliver by the creek, leaves bathing in the water, evening light dancing about his topmost branches. "There you are," I said, kneeling in his shadow. I rolled up my jeans and dipped my feet in the sun-warmed water, a swirl of minnows scattering with the ripples.

I watched an ant, tiny and determined and probably lost and lonely, crawl over the mountain ridges of my jeans. I named it *Deirdre*.

"Nearly died at the cliffs today," I told Oliver. "Got to see Inis Eala. You won't believe what happened." And I told him all about the swan and the locket, and when I finished, I said, "But it doesn't matter. Nuala won't let me visit the isle."

A breeze swept through the glade, and Oliver leaned in close. I remembered my ribbon and freed my hair for the wind to comb, then dug up a flat stone from beneath the grass and the brambles and the cool, soft dirt. "It just en't fair. If only she'd let me *try*, maybe . . ." I sighed and flung the stone down the creek, watched it skip three times before sinking like a shipwreck. "Maybe then she'd see I'm ready."

If Oliver could talk, I knew he'd take Nuala's side, even if he secretly agreed with me. After all, he always had. But that was the thing about talking with trees— unless you were completely off your nut, they didn't talk back.

I used to believe they did.

I snapped a leaf from Oliver and let Deirdre crawl onto it. I placed the leaf in the grass and began to gather some wildflowers—forget-me-nots, daisies, and foxgloves. I edged over to the knothole at Oliver's roots and laid the flowers there, just as Nuala had laid his ashes five years ago. "Now," I said, "if the swans come a-visitin' tonight, leave their tracks and leave their feathers. I s'pose I'll come by in the morning."

I stood, kissed my finger, and then laid the kiss on Oliver's bark, just like the flesh-and-bones Oliver used to do to my forehead. "See you," I whispered, and turned to leave.

"Who're you talkin' to?" The voice came from the tree. The *tree*.

My hand leapt for my chest, and I jumped back—fumbled, stumbled, tumbled—*splash*. Into the creek I fell. *Well*, I thought bitterly, splashing about in the water, *wasn't today just a festival of Finn Falling into Things.*

"Are you okay?" A rustling of leaves and branches sounded, and as I groped for the creek's edge, a freckled hand caught my own. I spluttered for breath as the hand yanked me to shore.

I spat a mouthful of creek water and coughed, "Yeah, yeah, I'm fi—*Darcy?*"

The child cast a bashful gaze to her feet—bare—and then knelt beside me. "Sorry," she muttered. "I didn't mean to—to startle you or anythin'."

I wrung out my hair and said, "No, I just thought you were—er—someone else. Never mind that—what're you doing here, hiding up in a tree? You should be back home with Sean and Mary. Weren't they s'posed to be looking out for you today? It en't always safe in the glades, you know. You could get lost, or slip on a rock and snap your ankle clean in two."

Darcy's mouth twitched. "So could *you*."

"Aye, but I'm twelve, and you're six, seven?"

"Seven and a quarter," said Darcy, tipping up her chin.

I peeled a string of seaweed off my jeans and said, "Matters not. Point is, you're just a little 'un, which means you've got to do like you're told. Understand?"

Darcy sighed. "Yes, Finn."

There was a familiar longing in Darcy's voice, and I realized perhaps I had inherited more of Nuala than her lily-pale hair and big feet. "Now, don't be down on yourself." I stood, sneakers slopping, and took Darcy's hand and pulled her up. "We'll walk home together. What were you doing in the glade anyway?"

"Lookin' for faery," said Darcy. She brushed off her skirt and added, "They say in the village, no one knows the faery better 'n you, Finn. 'Sides Nuala, of course. You were talking to one just then, weren't you? Have you seen 'em? Heard 'em?"

"No, Darcy."

Her face fell. "Oh."

I knelt down to Darcy's ear level and whispered, "I've felt 'em." Darcy's eyes ballooned. "Felt 'em in my own thumpin' heart, strong as the beat of a bodhrán drum."

We ducked under Oliver's waterfall of leaves and began to saunter through the glade, one squelching footstep after the next.

"Mary says I'm wasting me time out here," said Darcy. "She says they en't real, the faery."

I half smiled. "Neither are stories." But I leaned in close to her ear and whispered, "But that doesn't mean they don't exist." It was something Nuala had told me time and time again growing up. "And if you make a wish with all your heart and soul and do just as your da and Nanny Hurley and Father Cooley say, a faery'll come when you're 'specting it least and grant that wish for you. Did you know that?"

Darcy shook her head no.

Faery, of course, were not wish granters. They had their own troubles to deal with and their own wishes to tend to. But Darcy didn't know that, and the way I saw it, everyone deserved something to believe in, even if it wasn't real. I wanted to believe. I didn't have to, and I knew I was too old, but Darcy, *Darcy* of all people, needed that scrap of belief. She was, after all, the only other kid I knew whose father also worked for the Irish Republican Army in Belfast, and who didn't have a mother to boot. No one else could really understand what it was like to get used to the feeling of longing, always, for someone you didn't know would return or not.

"You know," I said, "these stones tell stories. Look here."

I took Darcy's hand and led her under an oak branch to a tall stone curtained behind a honeysuckle bush. The rock was worn smooth as the covers of my favorite storybooks; I'd seen many a time wayfarers stopping by just to touch, feel the stone. Liars, some

21

would say the ancient people were. Ignorant, some would say the ancient people were. Imaginative, some would say the ancient people were. Truth tellers, some would say the ancient people were. My own opinion floated like will-o'-the-wisps along the surfaces of those beliefs, hopping like skipping stones between each one. I wished on occasion that if I hung around Darcy enough, my belief would strengthen in the stories I had once so clung to like religion. Those stories were the threads that held Darcy and me together, but also the ones that pulled us apart.

"Look at the lines," I told Darcy. The stone was carved with the ancient script of Ogham, a series of scratches and scars, like wrinkles, like stories, like Nuala.

Darcy ran a muddy fingernail in one of the carved lines. "You can read this?" she breathed.

I nodded. "You read it bottom to top, like so," and I placed my finger at the bottom right corner, where the Ogham story started.

Darcy gazed up at me. "Well, what's it say? Is it a story? It's a story, en't it?"

"Aye, 'tis a story, but a cursed one." I plucked a

honeysuckle berry and squished it between my fingers, juice splattering down my jeans. "Some say it's the faery fruit of tales, ensnaring its victims into eternal wandering. I wouldn't wish such a fate on *anyone*. Nuala says any ear that catches but a drop of it becomes plagued with an unquenchable thirst to find the swans of—ah, I've said too much."

Darcy's eyes glittered bright and wide as the harvest moon. She shook her head of dark curls and gripped my sleeve, begging, "Tell it, Finn, please, please, *please*."

A pang of guilt clutched my stomach tight, but the actress in me could not resist a story, and it hurt the way *actress* was just another word for *liar*, but if I thought about it, was I lying? Were we storytellers simply glorified liars? Or underrated truth sayers? I did not know. "Oh, dear," I said, and sighing theatrically, I took Darcy's hand and began to meander through the trees again. "I suppose the damage has been done. Not a medicine in the world can cure it. Nothin' else to do but finish off the story."

Darcy beamed, and I began. "Once, in a green glade on a green isle, lived Lir, a man of all the riches in the world, but still, unhappy. He desired family. Madly in love with the daughter of a half faery, he married. In time, Lir's wife gave birth to three children with hair pale as seafoam, eyes dark as midnight, and lips red as hawthorn berries."

Darcy's eyes began to wander, so from a nearby hawthorn tree, I plucked a berry and dropped it into her palm. "But don't eat it," I warned. "For it is said that ever since this story came to close, those berries have remained as cursed as the children themselves, and if I finish, you will find out why. Ah, but I must be boring you with such old and dreary—"

"No!" piped Darcy. She held the berry at arm's length as if examining a particularly grumpy hermit crab. "No, I want to hear the rest."

"As you wish." I smiled and continued on. "These children were called Ena, Fiachra, and Conn. But . . . they came with a price, and that price was Lir's wife.

"'Lir,' his wife said as she cradled Conn for the first time, 'take care of 'em. Keep 'em close, always.' And then she died."

Darcy stopped in her tracks and dropped the hawthorn berry. "No."

"Aye. Lir buried his love himself in these very glades.

His only comforts rested in his children and his wife's sister, Aoife, who looked extraordinarily similar to his wife. So soothing was the sight of Aoife that Lir grew drunk with love."

"Like Mr. Quigley at the pub last Thursday?"

"No, Darcy, that's regular drunkenness. *Love-drunkenness* is a far worse affliction; but Lir's love was not for Aoife, rather the mirror of his parted wife he saw in her. Years later, wedding bells went a-ringin', and Aoife gave birth to a baby girl—Darcy."

Darcy's eyes grew large. It was a storytelling trick I'd learned from Nuala, who had always, forever, put my name in for Aoife's daughter. "*Darcy?*" gasped Darcy. "That en't true—can't be—*is* it?"

"Don't get your hair in a fluff, now; Darcy's hardly an uncommon name 'round here. 'Sides, if all's like the story says, Darcy had hair the color of raven feathers"—I squinted to make out Darcy's eye color—"and eyes like storm clouds over Connemara—oh my."

Darcy's mouth hung broad as the caves down by Maghera Beach. I patted her shoulder and said, "Best to give stories the benefit of the doubt. As I was telling, all was well. Aoife loved Darcy and cared for Lir's children like her own. But her love was not returned. The children, particularly Ena, were distrustful of Aoife, for they unraveled a most treacherous secret: Lir's first wife did not die of illness. Aoife killed her with her half-faery power of life."

"But . . . but that's a good power, en't it?" said Darcy.

"One would think. But Aoife did not grow beautiful things like flowers and dragonflies. She grew thornbushes, and one, she grew in her own sister's heart."

Darcy squirmed at the image.

"Of course," I continued, "Lir didn't believe the children, but they knew the truth. So Ena kept Darcy far at bay from Aoife, raising the baby as her own. Jealousy festered in Aoife, for Ena had not only taken her child, but also stolen Lir's attention. And jealousy, if sits for too long, spoils to bitterness, and bitterness spoils to spite. Well, Lir grew tired of—"

"Darcy." The voice came from nowhere, light, bright, and cloyingly sweet; it belonged to the sort of person who flicks fingers through candle flames, makes monkey faces at British guards, taps on lion cages at zoos. "He grew tired of Darcy—that's how it goes, en't it, Story Queen?"

I whirled around. A spidery boy stood there, unkempt

sooty hair sticking out at odd angles, and long eyelashes shadowing black-widow eyes. Between his pimpled nose and gangly legs, he could have passed for seventeen—but his pinched face and baby lips gave him away; he was hardly old as me. He tilted up an abnormally pointed chin and taunted, "Lil' Darcy's father grew tired of her and abandoned her for the more—ah—*venturous* life, didn't he? Go on, love, tell it like it is. The kid can handle it."

His spidery legs skirted around Darcy, and I grabbed Darcy's wrist, yanking her close. *"Don't* call me 'love,'" I spat. I knew he was talking about Darcy's real father, and I didn't like it, not one bit, so I added, "And there en't nothing 'venturous' about them riots—" But the boy cut me off.

"Nothing personal, 'course," he said. In one swish of a knobby hand, he grabbed a mosquito and crushed it between thumb and forefinger, then added, "Some men just grow bored of the humdrum provincial life. Love grows tired after—"

I stepped closer to the boy, his scrunched-up nose an inch from the top of my head. I stood on tiptoes to almost meet his eye level and growled, "Don't you dare—"

"Children." A smirk spread across his thin lips, and

anger brewed in the pit of my stomach.

I glanced to Darcy. Tears brimmed in her eyes, and I held her wrist tighter. "Who're you anyway?" I snapped. "You're a goer-through, en't you? Nothin' but a gypsy boy, here one day, gone the next."

I tried to push past him, but he blocked my way. "Aye, you're right on that one, love—"

"Don't—"

"I never stay in one place." He skittered around Darcy and me again and added, "Take three guesses why."

I rolled my eyes. "I'm not playing games with you. Now let us by."

"Ah-ah-ah," twitted the boy. "I think you'll be beggin' me just the opposite when you get a peek at this." Out from his pocket, he whipped a tarnished oval locket suspended by a thin chain speckled with blood. My hand leapt for my neck, traced the slight cuts the chain had drawn while pulling me up from the abyss of the Slieve League Cliffs. And as I edged closer to the boy, I found I could still smell Nuala's rosemary soap on the silver, wafting through the air.

That locket belonged to me.

Chapter 3

My mouth did jumping jacks as I fumbled for the precise words, the majority of which were not suitable for polite company—which wouldn't have been a problem if not for Darcy. "You *sneak*!"

The spidery boy clucked his tongue and chided, "Better watch that mouth, love, if you ever want to see this again," and he dangled the locket up out of my reach.

"Where'd you get that?" I demanded.

"Ah, so now I'm interesting," the boy sneered. "Well, it en't your business. S'pose it's mine now, huh?"

I put a hand on my hip, but Darcy spoke before I had a chance. "No *way*. It belongs to Finn, you boghead.

Don't it, Finn? That belongs to you. I've seen it 'round old Nuala's neck."

The boy shrugged. "Catch it if you can," he said, and then began to juggle the locket with the quick-handedness of a master magician.

I jumped and grabbed for the locket, but the boy dangled it up out of my reach. "Give it!" I yelped, suddenly regretting quitting my Irish dance lessons five years ago.

"Fish outa water, are you? What's that *smell*?" The boy crinkled his nose, his face becoming distinctly puglike. "Seaweed? Ah—no. River scum. Or is that just your armpits' scent *au naturel*? That means 'natural.'"

"I know what it means," I snapped. "And you're vile." I gritted my teeth as I jumped one more time, but then surrendered. "What do you want from me?" I searched in my pockets, but found only gum wrappers, a bus ticket from Belfast, and a hawthorn leaf named Grainne.

A wicked smile skulked in the corner of the boy's mouth. "A favor."

"And what might that be?"

The boy tipped up his chin precociously and said, "I want in. Take me with you to America."

Darcy gasped. "What a positively horrid trade. It en't hardly fair at all, for such a tiny trinket, an' Finn'll never take such an unfair trade, en't that right, Finn? Wait— America? What's America have to do with any—"

I hushed Darcy. I had a feeling the boy could have offered me to trade a bag of crisps for the locket, and Darcy still would have argued it wasn't fair.

But how boggling the boy's proposal was. I had never made plans of traveling to America, or even taken any interest in the idea. Perhaps he had gotten his information from Ciara Cassidy, a pinch-faced girl from school who enjoyed spreading nasty rumors about me. Ciara probably wished more than anyone that I was being shipped off to Boston or perhaps New York City, where they say there swarms so many people they blend together like crayons on hundred-degree pavement. And so I told the boy, "Well, luck's out. I en't going to America."

"Aye, but you will, love." He said it like he had a secret—a pickpocketed one at that.

I flapped my hands about and said, "Fine, whatever. Now, would you give me my locket?"

The boy complied and dropped Nuala's locket into my hands. It was unsettlingly warm with the heat of the boy's hand, and I rubbed it on my jeans to wipe away all traces of the boy. This was my and Nuala's treasure, no one else's. "Thanks," I muttered, and the boy shrugged.

But I wasn't stupid. As I clasped the chain around my neck, it occurred to me that the boy might have taken the photograph from inside. So, I carefully pinched the tiny door of the locket.

"Don't trust me, doll face?" chirped the boy.

"Not exactly, no," I said, scowling at him as I opened the locket. The photo was still there, but to my surprise, something else fluttered out from inside—a moth? A maple seed? A feather?

I caught my breath, my eyes widening as I bent to pick it up from the carpet of willow leaves. As I pinched the corner, however, I realized it was none of those things at all. Rough and brittle, it was a thin scrap of bark from a tree—a *hawthorn* tree.

"Not expecting that, were you?" said the boy.

I pocketed the scrap and stood, trying hard as possible to mask my surprise.

"I think Finn knows quite well what she keeps in her own locket," puffed Darcy. "En't that right, Finn?"

I nodded vaguely as a dizzying fog drifted through

my brain, wobbled my ankles. "R-right, Darcy. Er—time to get you home. C'mon."

Darcy's house was now in view, hardly a flea of a thing in the vastness of the green hills before us. I took her hand and pushed past the boy, but so irritating was he that he stuck out his big, floppy-booted foot in front of me, and I stumbled over it. "What *now?*"

"Not even a goodbye? How impeccably rude," said the boy.

"Bye," I said flatly, pushing past him, but he rounded Darcy and me again.

"I wanted to tell you one last thing, and I daresay you'll want to hear it." He waited for dramatic effect as I tapped my toe before continuing on. "Those swans en't gonna wait around forever," he said. "They en't gonna wait for the snow to fall, the grass to grow, the war to end, and they en't gonna wait for the dead to come home."

I shot a glance toward Darcy. Tears welled in her eyes, and for a second, I thought I saw a spidery-legged lough monster reflected in them—but no, it was just the boy. "Wh-what does he mean?" Darcy choked, grabbing my sleeve. "Waitin' for the dead?"

"Nothin'," I assured her. "He means nothin', and he's just about going anyway."

"I mean," said the boy, swiveling around me and curling over Darcy like a tarantula over its prey, "you can keep a lookout for your daddy at the top of that willow all you want, but he en't *never* comin' home."

A sputter much like that of a broken pipe escaped Darcy's throat, and she let go of my sweater. She staggered back, and I reached for her. "Darcy! Darcy, it en't true." But she had already started running. I shot a glare at the boy, then darted after her, calling, "Darcy, wait—"

But she was already down the hill and halfway through her garden. Sean and Mary—her teenage neighbors—stumbled out of their house at the sound of Darcy's wailing, and I could see even from far away their confused expressions.

I whirled around to face the boy. His cheeks were scrunched into a sickeningly pleased expression. "Now you've done it," I said.

The boy shrugged innocently. "All I'm saying is, if I was you, Finnuala O'Dálaigh-Sé . . . I would hop to it."

I hadn't told him my name. This time as I spoke, my voice trembled. "Hop to what?"

The boy leaned in close, and his eyes fell to my locket. "You can't let stories suffocate you. Sometimes, the trick is plain and simple as breathing underwater."

The trouble was, though, that there was nothing plain and simple about . . . But then I knew. How could I possibly have been so dense? It was *obvious*. The boy must have realized my understanding, because he gave a last crooked smile and swished off through the trees.

"Hey," I called, and I called thrice more, but it wasn't until I said, "What's your name?" that he paused and turned on his heel.

Something flitted about his eyes, something bright, something haunted—a will-o'-the-wisp, perhaps. The boy tipped up his chin and said, "Never mind my name."

But I did mind his name. Everything, big and small, sweet and foul, deserved a name. And so I named him. And I hadn't a clue whether he heard me or not, but once he was out of eyesight, I hollered, "I'll call you Sojourn." And that was that.

Chapter 4

MY MIND WAS ABUZZ. Getting to Inis Eala was easy; all I needed were the proper tools. I was about to take off through the forest, when I remembered the weight in my pocket. From within it, I pulled out the sliver of hawthorn wood and turned it twice in my hand, then once more. Something was written on the wood. The ink was red and dripping, and in splotchy, childlike handwriting, the wood read:

Meet me at the bleeding tree.

"Curious," I whispered, half to myself, half to the willows. The image of the blood-drop-berried hawthorn hanging off the edge of Inis Eala stuck in my mind.

Sojourn was right—I hadn't time to spare. Someone had left me a message . . . someone needed me to find them. Nuala's voice rang in my ears, *"You may go when you are needed there."*

So back through the willow glades I flew. Wind tearing at my hair, blisters ripping at my feet, I slowed my pace only upon catching sight of the scarlet door. Nuala said our home was like twilight—half of it drenched in sunlight, and the other half, darkness. This was because whoever built our cottage built it on the threshold of the willow glades, so everything west of the door was perpetually shadowed by a willow named Seamus.

"Lucky," Nuala called it many a time. She said so because this way, we always had a sunny spot to hang our laundry (and indeed, a line of jeans and patchwork sweaters hung like Christmas ornaments on the sunlit side), and a shady spot to tell stories and let the sheep sleep. But I knew the truth—I knew all halfway places were faery territory.

Panting, I traipsed through the wildflower garden (saying hello to the sheep, Maisie and Jack, along the way) and pulled open the door, bits of scarlet paint flying off from it and settling on the doorstep like autumn leaves. The door, too, was in a halfway place, rotting and weary, yet still strong enough to stay standing.

The kitchen was dark still, which meant Nuala wasn't home yet—perfect. I crossed the room, pots clinking and clanking with my big-footed steps, then whizzed up the narrow wooden staircase and into my room. I flicked on the glass lamp by my bed, wiped the dust from the window with my sleeve, and peered out to make sure Nuala wasn't toddling down the lane just yet. All was clear.

I had to find it. But where had I left it? I yanked shut my curtains and flung open the closet door. A thicket of odds and ends, baubles and knickknacks cluttered the top shelf. A swan-shaped pin Da had given me sparkled from the shelf. He never believed my stories, but he pretended to most days anyway. I reached up and loosened a yo-yo from beneath a stack of precariously piled books, and—

"*Aargh!*" I shielded my head as the trinkets came toppling down on me, clattering against the floorboards, a snow globe shattering into a thousand pieces.

I closed my eyes, held my breath—*one, two, three, four . . .* Silence.

I gave a sigh of relief; Nuala still wasn't back. I knelt down and mopped up the snow globe (along with a smattering of dried-up spiders) with an old first-grade choir sweater. Then I surveyed the rest of the trinkets: three paper airplanes, a box of seashells, a pair of Cinderella dress-up shoes, a ratty umbrella, and a blue marker-faced Barbie doll. So really, nothing.

I strained my memory. The last time I had it was five summers ago on holiday with Da. *If I were me five years ago, where would I put it?* I ran my hand along the top shelf, struggling to reach the back. My wee toe muscles strained to lift me higher, but it was simply too *tall* for me to—

Of course! I was hardly seven when I last used it; I would never have put it somewhere high. And with my aversion to packing and unpacking, I probably wouldn't have even put it away . . .

I slammed shut my closet and dove under the bed. *There.*

"Finn?"

My head snapped up, bopping against a metal rod of my bed frame. "Ouch!" I squealed.

"Are you in there?" The doorknob creaked.

"I'm naked!" was the only thing I could think to keep Nuala from bursting in. I cringed as Nuala simpered, "Oh?"

"Yes—hang on."

I shimmied out from under my bed, dust bunnies and cat hair clinging to my damp sweater, and lunged for my bathrobe. My big toe stubbed on the bedpost, and I rabbit-hopped about on one foot, fumbling for the edge of my bed before finally grabbing the bathrobe from my pillow. I flung it over myself, tied it at my waist, then bolted for the door as Nuala's voice rang, "Is everything all right in there?"

"Perfect!" and I threw open the door, hair flying.

Nuala scanned me up and down. A shooting star flecked across Nuala's dark eye, and I made a wish. *Please don't let her know. Please, please, please.* "Is the hot water running again?" she asked.

"Oh—" I glanced down to my bathrobe, and said, "Yes, yes, water's great. Stellar, really. Felt a tad muddy after visiting ol' Oliver, so I took a shower. That's why I'm wet."

"Ah, I see," said Nuala.

I admit, my stories were better than my lies.

"And," added Nuala, "you took the liberty of showering in your jeans and sweater to save a load of laundry?"

"Er—yes?" I answered, though it sounded more like a question.

Nuala beamed a mouthful of crooked teeth and plump gums. "My, how you outdo yourself, Finn," she said. And then her expression fell into a matter-of-fact one as she said, "You did get the berries? From Mrs. McLean?"

Crumbs. "They were fresh out." I crossed my fingers behind my back; I hated lying to Nuala—mostly because she could see straight through me.

"Oh. Oh, well, it's a good thing they, ah—*restocked* since you came back," and Nuala pulled a sack of black-berries from her overlarge sweater pocket.

My cheeks flushed, and my mouth waggled up and down in search of sorries, but Nuala spoke before I had a chance—and when she did, I was surprised to find her mouth was catching sorries too. "I'm sorry 'bout the swans, lass," she said, squeezing my hand and leading me over to my bed. There was something about her voice—the milk and honey of it—that put a stopper in any anger I felt.

We sunk into the patchwork quilt Nuala had sown with scraps from all the sorrows we knew. The corner was for Da, made from a piece of his first soldier uniform, greenish-brown and scuffed white with gunpowder. Beside Da's patch was Ma's—a handkerchief, yellow-blotted, and

41

smelling the way sea salt and tears do. Grandpa Oliver's patch was the only one I'd ever tasted, and my goodness did I regret it. I had thought it was flecked with cinnamon, but had the misfortune of discovering the flavor of cayenne pepper, which, apparently, Grandpa Oliver had rather enjoyed with his eggs Benedict on Sunday mornings.

The patch beneath Grandpa Oliver's was what had once been a flowery patch, but now was only a pathetic smudge of charcoal, which Nuala said was for nothing, but she wasn't the only one clever at reading lies. The rest were for my friends and for Nuala's friends, people who had come and gone, but mostly gone. People didn't stick around too much in our village, Carroway. It was more the sort of place you went through to get somewhere else. It was a halfway place, and faery or not, my heart didn't take too kindly to that.

Nuala trilled her nails along Grandpa Oliver's cayenne patch like she was playing his old grand piano—the one now rotting in the cellar. Then, with nimble fingers, she untied the sack of blackberries and offered them to me. I took a berry, the sweet and sour stinging but soothing my tongue, which had shriveled dry from my story to Darcy and my argument with Sojourn.

"Let's do something fun," said Nuala unexpectedly. "Get both our minds off the swans."

I looked up to Nuala. I knew her wrinkles by heart, and so I also knew an extra one had appeared above her brow— that was her worry wrinkle. I didn't want to worry Nuala, but I also didn't want to keep my mind off the swans, and now I certainly had no intention of going anywhere but Inis Eala tonight. So, I said, "That's okay, Nuala—really, I'm fine. I'll see the swans another year. It's no big deal."

Nuala sighed and popped a blackberry into her mouth. She gulped it down, and breathed, "You'll be a brave one, lass? For me?"

I looped my ankles around each other and muttered, "Not much bravery about stayin' out of trouble's way, if that's what you mean."

"There is a difference between being brave and being rash, my love." That was the same thing she told Da before he'd run off to the riots in Belfast, even though to me, Da was the bravest person I knew. Nuala brushed the black-berry juice off her hands and adopted a tone of more finality than I really cared for. "Well, then," she said, "come on down when you're ready. We're going to McCann's for supper tonight. My treat."

"Er—no thanks. I actually—I thought I might visit Darcy. You know, Mr. Brannon's little girl. I'll sleep over there. Her nanny won't mind, and I can cook myself some toast or something simple. 'Sides—I—I may've finally got a friend, and she's really quite n—"

"That wasn't a question, Finn. I said we're going to McCann's, now dry up." Nuala stood and turned for the door as I stammered, "But—but—"

"Not a word, Finn," said Nuala sternly, and her gaze was hemlock-laced enough for me to know to hush up.

I nodded, and Nuala cracked open the door. But before stepping out, she swiveled around and added delicately, "Oh—and Finn?"

"Mm?"

Nuala's eyes sparkled like fireworks. "Always hide your evidence."

I followed Nuala's gaze to my snow-globe-soaked sweater and felt my heart spin to sheep's wool. My mouth played hopscotch with my brain, but Nuala left before I could explain—not that I had reason to. Nuala knew precisely what I was up to. Not a single explanation was needed. Just a better plan.

THE MINUTE NUALA LEFT, I dove beneath my bed. A snorkel the color of marigolds—very dusty, very *spidery* marigolds—sat wedged inside a pair of mud-caked sneakers four sizes too small. The snorkel, too, looked four sizes too small, but it would have to do.

Nuala would surely have her ears perked for my footsteps and one eye open for my shadow all night long if need be. Nonetheless, I snatched the snorkel and wriggled out from under my bed, coughing up a puff of dust like Mr. McCann did when he smoked, leaning footcrossed against his pub.

I grabbed my periwinkle knitted pouch from my bedpost, the dulcet lilt of seashells chinking from inside. When I pulled the drawstrings open, the smell of seaweed filled my nostrils, and I stuffed the snorkel inside. I yanked open my bedside table drawer, the glass lamp atop it teetering hazardously. I rummaged through a hodgepodge of mismatched buttons and old gum wrappers until I found it.

The leather ran soft on the cover and ragged on the spine, splotched with ink and sap and even a spot of marmalade. On the front were the words, scribbled in my wobbly six-year-old handwriting:

A field journal of folk, faery,

and other findings:

Property of finnuala rose o'dálaigh-sé

And then in the bottom right-hand corner:

No peeking—that means YOU!

Except for me, of course. I flipped it open, the cover crackling like embers, and leafed through the iris-wrinkly pages to a section labeled "My Swans." The words were tapestries of fact and fiction, threads sewn together to create something that made sense and didn't make sense all in one. The swans section was the fattest in the whole book and was cluttered with bookmarks. I pulled out each bookmark, leaving only the one with the dragonfly key chain marking the swan section, so I could find it easily. When I finished, I crammed the book into my pouch with the snorkel. Operation Story-Hunting was underway.

Chapter 5

AFTER QUICKLY CHANGING FROM MY JEANS into my one-and-only skirt and tying up my hair with my scarlet ribbon, I slung the pouch over my shoulder and met Nuala under Willow Seamus.

"All right, Finn?" she said.

"As I'll ever be," I said, trying hard as possible to sound defeated despite the determination burning in my chest like a Beltane bonfire.

"Chin up, lass," piped Nuala, tapping up my chin. "Mr. McCann's got a hot cider with your name on it," and we sauntered out of the willow glades and down the path to the village. The term *village* was used loosely; all it meant was that it was more populated with people than sheep.

A twisty dirt road wound through a garden of shops and houses popping up in random spaces like buttercups. The entire town was but one strip of colored buildings winding through a field of the greenest grass one could possibly fathom. Nuala's you're-lucky-if-it's-open quilt shop sprouted like a primrose, pink and cozy things peeking out from the windows. Rain-washed flowers drooped from windowsills and the scent of Mrs. Pilkin's scones wafted through the air. But what I loved most about Carroway were the doors, which, on sunny days, were more open than not.

That, and McCann's. McCann's Pub was like my favorite pair of sneakers—ragged and weathered and all together wonderful. A stark-white ramshackle place it was, thatched roof, cracked windows threatening to shatter any minute, and the red of the door splintering to the under-brown. Clearly, Mr. McCann cared not for finery, but coziness. And so did I.

Music bled through the chips in the windows, and the tap of dance shoes against walnut wood thundered my heart. As Nuala and I crossed the threshold, a burly man raised a glass in our direction. "Ah, our storytellers," he bellowed, taking a swig of Guinness.

"Nuala, Finn!" chirped Mr. McCann from behind the bar. A crooked smile broke his dry and scabby face. "Hot cider and a Baileys comin' right up," and he swished a rag across a place for two at the bar.

We sat on the bar stools, feet dangling, as Mr. McCann sloshed our drinks across the counter. The fiddler sped up his tune as Nuala's fingers tapped in time against her glass, and the dancers quickened their feet. Though the thick crowd blocked my view of them, I could tell their speed by the *clack-click-a-clacking* of their shoes, triple time now. A last warble trilled from the fiddle around the tavern, and the dancers stomped to a finish.

The pub erupted into cheers, clinking glasses and clapping shoulders. A small figure weaseled through the throng. Her black curls clung to her face with sweat, and her dance shoes weighed down her bony legs like plump apples sprouted from twigs.

"Ah, Darcy, my love, that's a smashing show you give," applauded Mr. McCann to the dancer, dusting out a glass. "How 'bout a cider for you, on me?"

"Thanks, Mr. McCann," said Darcy, hopping up to a bar stool beside me.

I turned to her and said, "Cheered up a bit?"

Darcy nodded; she never stayed upset for long. Then I added, "I didn't know you were dancin' tonight."

"Bridget's got the summer flu," replied Darcy, "so Miss Eileen asked me to step in." She took a gulp of cider, then sleeve-wiped away the golden mustache brimming her mouth. "What're you an' Nuala doing here? What's that pouch for an' why's it smell like seaweed? You know, I really *did* want to hear the rest o' that story you were tellin', but you look like you're about to leave for some—"

Nuala had raised her eyebrows, and I swiftly lifted my glass and hollered, "Who's up for a story?"

To my relief, a roar of "Mes" and "Absolutelys" and "Yes pleases" muffled Darcy's questions. No one could resist a story told by Nuala, as if she were a silver-tongued faery, lips spilling rubies and gold. And then, silence settled upon the pub like fresh fallen snow. The weight of two dozen ears compressed my bones, and my neck began to shrink into my shoulders. Tortoises, I decided, were very lucky creatures indeed.

I cleared my throat, turned from Darcy, and babbled, "Fantastic. Er—Nuala—why don't you tell that one about the ravine?" Storytelling for Darcy or Grandpa Oliver or even Mr. McCann was one thing, but a whole *pub*—I left that to Nuala, thank you very much.

Nuala batted a hand and laughed. "That old one again? I must'a spent more of me life tellin' that tale than brushing my teeth."

"Oh, come on, *please*," groaned a porky man, and a tidal wave of begging washed over the pub.

Nuala frowned wryly at me before complying. "Very well." She perched her feet on the stool's ledge and leaned in close. "Once, in a world weary with troubles, there yawned a village of little remark—except, of course, for the ravine that gurgled at the edge of the wood. These waters were pricked by magic, reflecting not one's face, but one's true soul. Two sisters bathed in this ravine often, and the water reflected upon them truly—the elder, graced with eyes blue as serenity, and the younger, with hair yellow as joy. Their love for each other was simple, yet pure. A stronger sisterhood, not a sleuth could find. That was, until—"

The door flung open. The racks of glasses behind the bar shivered as a gust of wind billowed through the pub. A figure, big-footed boots and breathless, stood square in the doorway.

"Good heavens," said Mr. McCann, an empty glass falling from his hands onto the old oak bar. "Is it—"

But before he could finish his sentence, my voice crackled at the back of my throat, ". . . Da?"

Chapter 6

Da had a scar by his upper lip that winked when he smiled. He had one by his eyebrow, too, that hadn't been there the last time I'd seen him three months ago. "Baby girl," was what he said, beaming. He barreled through the crowd, lifted me from the barstool, and swung me thrice around in a flying waltz.

A few older ladies cooed, and Ciara Cassidy and her friends snickered. But right then, right then, it was just me and Da, and to me, Da's smile was a lighthouse, and I a fishing boat wandering the sea.

As my toes brushed the ground, however, Da's smile faded.

"What is it?" I said.

Da looked through me, and I turned, following his gaze.

"Darcy Brannon," he whispered.

Darcy hopped off her barstool, the click of her dance shoes echoing around the pub. "Yes?"

Darcy's nanny, Miss Hurley, bustled through the crowd to Darcy's side and gazed anxiously up at Da. Da pulled off his military hat and whispered, "I'm sorry."

My stomach plummeted. Miss Hurley's eyes widened and Mr. McCann's freshly poured copper drink teetered in his hand, then splashed onto the floor. Every eye turned to Darcy. It was as if everyone in the pub knew except for her.

"But, Mr. O'Sé," said Darcy, "I don't understand. You haven't done nothin'."

And then came the voice. That whiny, nose-stuck-in-other-people's-business, jumping-spider voice. It slithered soft and slowly into my and Darcy's ears, a harsh whisper like that of a rattlesnake's tail. Snakes had been banned from Ireland from Saint Patrick thousands of years ago. I wondered how Sojourn managed to get in. "He's dead, dummy. Dead, dead, dead. Dead as a doornail, dead as your Christmas tree in July. I won't say I told you so, but—"

"Shut up."

All eyes blinked to me. Goose bumps dappled my arms, and I slunk backward, wishing again I could be a tortoise.

Sojourn appeared in the corner of my vision, flanked by Ciara and her friends. How Sojourn had already weaseled his way into Ciara's crew was beyond me. And as I shrunk back farther, Sojourn tipped up his chin and shrugged. "Someone had to tell her."

I huffed and shook my head, then surprising myself, I spat, "You're pathetic, you know that?"

I grabbed Darcy's wrist and yanked her through the crowd. She limped faintly along as if her limbs were filled with helium. We stumbled into a back room cluttered with cardboard boxes smelling of stale whisky. Another door behind a large box had a sign hanging lopsided by a single nail atop it, reading EXIT.

"Just through here," I muttered, and pulled Darcy along outside.

The door led to an alleyway where the walls were dim and the moon was bright. Bright and big and hollow—a mirror of Darcy's eyes.

I forgot I owned a tongue as I struggled for words. But then Darcy seemed to remember her own tongue.

And she screamed. The night held its breath. Darcy slumped down against the pub wall, her fingers slipping from mine.

And all I could do was stare. Because looking at her was like realizing for the first time that wishing stones don't work on you. That what you want has nothing to do with what you deserve, and what you deserve has nothing to do with what you get. Because happily-ever-afters . . . they didn't exist for kids like us. I was a story-teller, and I knew that happily-ever-afters didn't exist in golden castles, and they didn't exist in enchanted forests. They didn't exist in life, and they didn't exist in death, and they sure didn't exist in stories. Happily-ever-afters took flight in dreams. And me and Darcy, we had impossible dreams. Wingless dreams. So really, we didn't even stand a chance.

And so I cried. I cried and cried and cried, and I didn't even know it before I was slumped next to Darcy, whispering, *"Shh, shh, shh . . ."*

When her sobs quieted, I propped my head on my hand and tried: "He was a good man. Kind and brave— really brave, like—like fire-breathing-gryphadragon brave."

That would normally have made Darcy giggle, but instead, tears pooled in her eyes. I fluttered my hands, but my fingers were like butterflies trying to hold back tidal waves. "No—no, that's not what I meant." I should have just kept quiet. "He's more like a—a Pegasus?"

"How does it end?" Darcy's voice caught me off guard. It sounded different. *Bad* different. She used to sound little, and now she sounded old as me, maybe even older.

"How does what end?" I whispered.

Darcy sniffed away a lingering sob. "Your story. The Children of Lir."

"Oh," I said, struggling to remember where we left off. But then I decided it didn't really matter where. Anywhere you started, it ended up in the same place. "The children turn to swans," I said.

Darcy blinked. "That's it?"

I patted my knee, and Darcy crawled onto it. I wrapped an arm around her and nodded. "The children's stepmother tried to murder them, and they turned to swans—all except Darcy. Darcy grew and grew, and one day in a willow glade, she heard the tale of the Children of Lir. And ever since, she spent her days searching for her long-lost half-siblings-turned-swans."

Darcy and I sat in silence for some time, Darcy staring up at me, still waiting for another piece of story. Finally, as the moon tiptoed over the edge of the alley walls, Darcy asked, "Well—well does she ever find 'em?"

I leaned close to Darcy's ear and whispered, "Some say she still roams these lands. That the story's still happenin' to this very day. Others, well, they say her search has just only begun. But not a storyteller in Ireland will say she's found them. It matters not, though, because that is where the story leaves us. There is not a whisper more."

"Well, I like it," decided Darcy. "Even if it is sad."

"Then it's yours."

Darcy peered up, and I added, "You're the first person I ever told that story. So that makes you the story's keeper. Like how I keep Nuala's stories. You know, one day, I'm gonna be a storyteller—a real one—just like her."

"Oh," said Darcy. "So who's gonna be your story keeper? For the rest o' the stories, I mean."

I rested my head back against the wall and thought. My whole life all I had wanted was brothers and sisters, and a mother, and a father who stuck around, or even just some friends, just like the girl in "The Children of Lir"— that and the swans, of course. And somehow, the two dreams were entwined. It wasn't like I believed the swans were my siblings or anything. It was just like . . . like if I found the swans, perhaps my dream of finding a real family of my own wouldn't seem so impossible. Perhaps I wouldn't feel so hopeless. Or so alone. And I knew I wasn't *really* alone—I had Nuala and Grandpa Oliver, even if he was a tree, and the hawthorn leaves and the sheep and the ants and Inis Eala and Da when he showed up. But still, more often than not, I, as sure as rain over Dublin, felt alone.

Except for Darcy. *Except for Darcy, except for Darcy, except for Darcy.*

I shook away the thoughts and said, "Here." I reached behind my neck and unlatched the clasp of the silver locket. "This is yours for the night. You need it more than me."

"Your locket?"

I nodded. "That way, you can keep me right here." I laid a finger on Darcy's chest, felt her heart *thump-a-thump-a-thump.* "You shouldn't have to be lonely tonight."

I fixed the locket around Darcy's neck as she said, "Oh."

"Something wrong?" I said.

"Well, it's just . . . what about you?"

"What about me?"

"You shouldn't have to be lonely, either."

"I'm not—"

"*I'm* not stupid. Besides, it's only fair you get something too. You need . . ." Darcy pulled her foot to her nose and leaned in close, fiddling with something on the side of her dance shoe. When at last she tore it from the leather, she held up the tiny, glittering object to the moon and announced, "*This.*"

I smiled wryly. "A shoe buckle."

"No," said Darcy, placing the silver buckle in my palm. "It's a wing. Miss Eileen says that's how we leap so high when we do our jumps at dance. Tie it to your ankle, you'll see," and Darcy unlaced a shoelace from her shoe, then looped it through the buckle and around my ankle.

I grinned and flourished my ankle so the starlight caught the metal. "How do I look?"

Darcy, puffy-faced and red-eyed, beamed. "You're perfect."

Chapter 7

DA SAT AT THE KITCHEN TABLE hunched over a cup of chamomile tea. The table looked doll-sized compared to his long legs, and the little wooden chair wobbled as he stirred his spoon. Nuala rattled around the pots and pans as Da waved her off. "I'm fine, Missus," said Da. He never got around to calling Nuala *Nuala* after he married Ma, but *Mrs. O'Dálaigh* was simply too long, so *Missus* worked just fine. "No need to fuss—"

"Don't be ridiculous," admonished Nuala, pouring a cup of oats into a rusted pot. The blue fire below the stovetop whizzed to life as she added, "Your stomach's probably shrunk to the size of a pea with all they feed you in the army."

"It's Belfast, Missus, not Vietnam," said Da. "We feed ourselves, and I get food plenty. If you want to pity someone, pity 'em soldiers down in the elephant grass and the orange gas. If you've got to pity someone close by, pity the young. Pity the church. Pity the land. Pity the sad and pity the angry. But me? Don't pity me."

I watched it all from the reflection of the window. My elbows tingled with the draft creeping under the ledge. I watched a spider tiptoe along the edge of the moon. Da's bravery was like a wing I wanted to borrow. Everything I'd always wanted.

Nuala sashayed across the kitchen with a steaming ceramic bowl. "Well, pity party aside, you're eating your porridge." She set it down before Da, then ruffled up his bangs and added, "Never mind your stomach, anyway— when was the last time you got a haircut? I'll do it in the mornin', now eat up."

Da shook his head, but didn't argue. He sprinkled five spoons of sugar and poured half a glass of cream into his porridge, then sighed, "*Mmm*. Like biscuits in a bowl."

"You're so gross, Da," I said, but my lips curled up.

"Ah, so she does speak," said Da. "Does she laugh too?" And he stuck out his porridge-speckled tongue.

"Lorcan," scolded Nuala.

I grimaced into the window as Da sheepishly stuck back in his tongue.

After he swallowed, Da squinted his eyes into his window reflection as if trying to stare into mine. "Pack's gettin' pretty heavy?" That was what Da said when he knew I was getting sad from other people's sadness. He said it because of a story I once told him (that Nuala once told me) about a peddler's mule that carried so many saucepans and whisky bottles and umbrellas and fiddles and teakettles and garden rakes upon his back that a wee straw buckled his knees and sent him tumbling into a valley.

Da put down his spoon and his tone grew serious as he said, "You don't have to carry everyone's sadness."

Oh, but I do, I thought. At least, I had to carry Darcy's.

Nuala swished over to me and kissed the top of my head. "If nothin' else is sure in this world, it's that our girl's got Aobh's heart."

The sound of my mother's name trilled against my heart like fingers on harp strings. Nuala pronounced it like *eve*, and that was how I imagined her, even though I'd only met her once, and I was only zero days old then. My mother was an eve: she was the magic that comes before Christmas morning, the chills that scuttle up your spine when something magnificent is just about to happen, the breathlessness that crashes upon you on the edge of wonder.

Da grinned. "Her heart, and her eyes, and her nose, and her toes, and her . . . *tickle spot*!" With a clatter of the too-small table, Da lunged, Nuala cupping his porridge bowl, and before I could quick-hop away, Da was at my ribs. I gasped with laughter and balled up like a roly-poly bug on the wood floor.

"Stop, stop!" I giggled, and Da retreated, sitting criss-cross on the floor opposite me. His scar smile stretched wider than I'd seen it stretch in a long time. Even Nuala muffled a laugh.

It was one of those moments that made me believe, truly, that all was beautiful and nothing could hurt us. Because even though joy wasn't permanent, sadness wasn't either, which was one of those sneaky, slippery secrets of the world. And I felt better for knowing it.

I wrangled in my laughter, but before my smile could fall any lower, Da said, "Are you hungry? You, baby girl, look absolutely *famished*."

"Actually, I'm fi—"

Da reached into his pocket and whipped out a little bag of sunshine-yellow candies.

"Lemon drops!" I grabbed the bag, tore it open, then handed out a round of lemon drops to Da, Nuala, and myself. As I popped mine into my mouth, the sour whizzed around my mouth, zinging off my tongue to the back of my throat . . . and then the sweet set in, buttery soft.

This, I thought, would be a perfect time to ask what had been pecking at the back of my brain all evening. Da was happy. Nuala was happy. Da was happier—my best bet. "Da?" I said. "You know who could *really* use a lemon drop tonight?"

"Who?" said Da.

"Darcy Brannon." I twirled my finger 'round a hole in my sleeve. "Can I sleep over at her house tonight? Miss Hurley wouldn't mind—I'm sure of it. Please?"

Simultaneously, Da said, "Sure," and Nuala said, "No." They exchanged glances. Nuala frowned. "*No*," she repeated, bulging her eyes out at Da.

"Of course she can go," exclaimed Da, getting to his feet. I got to mine as well and slunk to the table, lowered into the wobbly chair.

"Lorcan, you don't understand—"

"Is this how you're handling Finn's upbringing? Locking her up like some sunlight-deprived damsel?"

"I'm doing what I've done for the past eleven years, Lorcan—keeping her safe."

"Twelve years," whispered Da. "And don't you forget about the lost ones I cared for till they went missing under *your* care, Nuala."

I wasn't quite sure what Da was on about, and he muttered, "Sorry. Shouldn't 'a brought that up."

Nuala sighed and rubbed her neck, but Da's mouth crinkled with suppressed anger. "Finn is twelve years of age today, which is plenty old enough to spend a night away. And besides that, she's my daughter."

The wrinkles on Nuala's forehead deepened. "Lorcan, I promise you, I would allow her out any night except—"

"Her birthday? The night she should be off making prank phone calls and playing spin the bottle and stuffing herself with cake?"

I pretended to be intently fascinated with Da's sugar porridge and began to stir the spoon. When Nuala spoke, her voice was cold as the Skellig Islands in December. "She's *twelve*, not twenty-two—and she likes pie, not cake. And she has celebrated. She celebrated half the evening at McCann's until *someone* showed up—"

I shifted around in my chair and peered up at Nuala and Da, stomach squirming. "It's okay, I, er—I don't need to g—"

Da raised a hand and fired, "No, Finn, you're *going*." He turned back to Nuala, eyes narrowed. "My daughter, my rules. End of discussion."

Nuala huffed. "Have it your way, then. But when she's not around come mornin', this is on you—"

"Oh, don't be so melodramatic—"

"And once you run off again to Belfast, just know that *I* will be the one who weeps. Because Finnuala is more a daughter to me than she will ever be to you."

"Nuala—" I started, but Nuala ignored me. Wouldn't even look at me. And she strode past Da straight out the kitchen. Da took after her, bumping his head on a low-hanging pot, bellowing, "I'll die before somethin' happens to Finn—" but Nuala had slammed her bedroom door.

Da turned back, lips pursed and fists clenched.

"Da?" I whispered.

He wouldn't look at me, either. Something like a diamond glittered beside his eye. "Go pack, Finn." His voice cracked on my name.

"It's okay if—if I don't go—"

He marched over to where I sat at the table, swiped up the porridge and tossed it into the sink. "For God's sake, Finn, go pack your toothbrush and pj's and go to your friend's house." He leaned over the sink, head bowed.

I stood and made way for the staircase, but before I could scurry up, Da spoke. Didn't turn, didn't look, but spoke. "You *are* my daughter, baby girl. And I think about you always."

Chapter 8

GUILT TUGGED AT MY FINGERS, prying them off my hair-brush; I dropped it into my yellow duffel bag. I tossed my toothbrush, a couple of mismatched socks, a nightgown, and a pillow in too, and then I opened up my periwinkle pouch. Both the snorkel and my field journal flopped onto my quilt. My heart stuttered. *This is it. This could be my only chance . . .*

I buried the book and snorkel in my pillowcase, then zipped shut the duffel bag. I was ready.

MISS HURLEY'S FACE was puffed and white as a winter sheep. She dabbed her swollen eyes with a kerchief and hurried me inside the Brannons' farmhouse. She took my arm and led me through a daisy-wallpapered corridor, saying tenderly, "Ah, m'dear, the look on Darcy's face when she sees you . . ."

We arrived at a weathered white door, a line of green and pink alphabet stickers at the top reading:

D RCY

Miss Hurley tapped on the wood.

No answer.

"Darcy," tried Miss Hurley.

No answer.

"Darcy, love, I know you're upset, but 'tis no way to treat a guest."

The door cracked open and a black-lashed eye poked out—and then Darcy tumbled out of the room and into my arms. I dropped my duffel bag and held her close. When she retreated, she said nothing, but took my hand and led me into her room.

"If you girls need anythin', give me a holler," said Miss Hurley, and she closed the door.

There was not a spot of wall to be seen in Darcy's room. Dance ribbons and photographs and Christmas tree lights cluttered every inch. Darcy sat me down on the bed and began to sort a pile of stuffed animals. "You can sleep with Queen McSnuffagles and Mr. Pigglebean," she said, handing me a floppy-winged puffin and a ratty pig. "And I'll sleep with Chewy and Chomp—oh, and Persnickety Kettle, o' course. She gets pouty when I don't pick her." She squeezed a pair of matching goats and a too-stuffed cat against her chest, then looked up to me. "What d'we do now?"

I thought for a moment, stroking Mr. Pigglebean's ears. It occurred to me that I had never been to a sleepover before, unless our class trip to the Dublin Historical Museum counted, where we slept overnight with the deer skeletons and the badger bones. "Well, we could eat popcorn—"

"'Cept we don't have the corn to pop."

"Right, well, we could have a pillow fight—"

"'Cept my pillows are made o' goose feathers, and with goose feathers, you never know when one's gonna shoot out of the pillowcase and stab you in the eye or somethin'. Goose feathers are sharp at the ends, y'know."

"Right, well, we could—"

"Finish the story?"

"What story?"

"'The Children of Lir,' o' course!"

"I did finish it. Back at McCann's, don't you remember?"

"I want to hear it properly. All the details, not a button or a mouse or a hiccup left out." Darcy lay back on the bed, plopped Persnickety Kettle on her stomach and stared at me expectantly.

I sighed and snuggled up next to Darcy, pulling a pink crochet blanket up to our necks. I gazed up to the Christmas tree lights, winking on their wire, and thought back to the way Nuala had first told me the story. I was four years old, sitting on the stoop and feeding stale bread to the sheep when Nuala swished out from the back lilting, "Did you ever see a swan so pale and bright its feathers could be sewn of starlight? Did you ever see a child so red-lipped and pure its soul could be stitched of rosebuds and allure?"

And so I told my Darcy those very words. And then I told her everything. I told her all about how after Lir abandoned his second wife, Aoife (for she was a cruel woman, despite loving Lir's and her own daughter), he took all four of his children and allowed Aoife but one visit a year on the baby's birthday. How on that one visit, Aoife took the children for a visit to their grandmother who lived on an isle. How, as the older children, Ena,

Fiachra, and Conn, bathed in the water, Aoife tried to take her baby away.

And then I told Darcy of the hawthorn berries. The magic ones plucked from the tree at the edge of the tallest cliff of the isle. *"Eat these,"* Aoife told the children as they raced up the cliff to her and their baby sister. *"Eat these, or your precious sister dies."*

And they ate them. I told Darcy how the children fell to the ground, asleep, but before death had a chance to snatch them away, Aoife's mother, the half faery, found them. And in the in-between hour of dreaming and awake, the half faery cured the children with another berry plucked from the same tree—though these were blessed with love. But blessed as they were, the berries could not fully undo the curse unless eaten by she who had caused the curse. So, the children were revived, but at a price.

"They were to spend the rest of their lives as an animal," I told Darcy. "The half faery looked upon her grandchildren, so beautiful, even in near-death sleep, almost like royals."

I told Darcy how first, the half faery considered the children be turned to brave lions, for lions are rulers of the land. But, surely, they should rule the sea too, and she considered they be turned to gentle blue whales, for blue whales are rulers of the sea. But what about the sky? Surely, the children should rule the sky, and she thought for moment of turning them into proud eagles.

But then, as she gazed out over the shores of her isle, the half faery spotted a swan soar down from the heavens, glide along the sea, then step onto the shore to groom its feathers.

"So thus it was," I said. "The children would be swans, for swans are rulers of sky, land, and sea." The enchantment was cast, and away flew the swans.

The half faery banished Aoife from Ireland, then told Lir that his children had drowned, all but the baby. "And ever since, the youngest child spent her days searching, searching for her long-lost siblings-turned-swans." And as I spoke the last word, sleep, the sly creature, pinched shut Darcy's eyes.

My eyes, too, closed, but I did not sleep. I listened. Not a sound from the corridor, not a sound from the kitchen; Miss Hurley had gone to bed.

I opened my eyes, braced my feet for the floor. The springs of the mattress screeched as I pulled myself up. One footstep—loud as shattering glass. Another step—

loud as the sea smashing at the Burren. Still, Darcy slept on, and I knelt down to my duffel and pulled open the zipper, one zip at a time. I poked my head into my pillow-case and carefully withdrew the snorkel and field guide. And then out the creaking door I crept.

Chapter 9

THE WILL-O'-THE-WISPS must have been shy that night, for I hadn't a drop of light to guide my way. A cloud had drifted over the moon—storm or benevolent, I knew not. Usually I could tell the weather forecast by a glance to the oaks—turned-up leaves and thunder was to come—and the light of the place—greenish brought wind, bluish brought rain, grayish brought snow, and pinkish brought sunshine.

But of course there was no light, and I could not see the trees, and even the wind was strange, prickly against my skin, yet quiet as snowfall—not one tree shivered with the silent gusts. And I admit, though Nuala took me out to the edge of the willow glades to watch the stars or catch some fireflies, I was not as nimble with the woods and the fields, and oh the godforsaken *fences*, as I was in daylight.

My toes stubbed against stones, and my face thwacked against branches, and my hair tangled in bushes; but still, I carried on, running faster now, *pat-a-pat-a-pat-a* through the thistle. I veered west as well as I could tell, and a lullaby my father used to sing me hiccuped in my ears—hiccupped because Da often feigned the hiccups halfway through just to wake me up and make me laugh. But little did he know I had been feigning too—sleep, that is. And I would tackle him in tickles until his laughter grew wheezy. The lullaby would go: *West for the sea, West for the swans, West for the stories that carry me away.*

Soon, the wind breathed her true colors, rumbling louder and louder with each footstep I took. It boxed my ears like a mother scolding her child, and just as I was sure my skin was tearing off with the force of it, something wet caught my foot. For a foolish second, I believed I had reached the ocean at last, but no. There was no sand, and as the wind cooled its temper, I could hear that this water was not seawater at all, but creek water, water ruled by the faery Belisama. This water bubbled over stones and gulped at the dirt walls of its narrow passage.

My foot slid on a stone, but I caught hold of a branch to stop myself from completely falling in—I'd had enough falls for one day, thank you very much. The branch's tree lurched as I reeled myself out and collapsed on a bed of wildflowers, softer than heather. *Forget-me-nots, daisies, foxgloves.* I knew their scents by heart.

I scrambled to my feet and reached blindly toward the tree. Its bark ran coarse beneath my fingers, but seemed to smooth with my touch. Or perhaps my fingers were simply numbed with the chill of the creek water. Yet still, I recognized the wrinkles, recognized them as well as I would the ones over Nuala's brow.

"Grandpa Oliver," I whispered, giving the willow a hug. As I leaned over a branch I supposed would be akin to Oliver's elbow, something caught my eye. Now, I only saw it because, while the night was black, black, black, *this*, this was *white, white, white*. Pale like starlight.

"You kept your promise," I said, grinning to Oliver, then scurried over to the swan feather tucked in his roots and glistening seemingly on its own accord. Soft as the water sprung from the Wicklow Mountains, the feather glided through my fingers.

And then another one dropped into my vision, a white flame at the bend of the creek. Of course. By this point, I felt rather stupid. How could I forget? The creek emptied into the sea. All I had to do was follow the flow of the water.

I spun in a circle with joy (whopping my forehead on a branch), blew Grandpa Oliver a kiss, and hurried on to the next feather. At last, I had a steady path. So onward I traveled, collecting feathers like breadcrumbs from a story I knew long ago.

By the time the rushing of the ocean crashed into earshot, I had figured out that I was following the flight of not one, but three swans. I had also figured out that I must have had seen these particular swans' feathers before, for in my field guide, I had taped perfect twins. With every new feather, my field guide grew fatter until I hadn't a spare page to stuff any more.

As the smell of salt wafted down from the treetops, I became aware of the shoe buckle bopping against my ankle. *Flight.* The word rang in my ears, echoing from all four corners of the ocean slipping into view.

The ground became rockier, and I descended a stone-carved staircase until my feet hit the sand. I pulled out my orange snorkel and dropped my field journal on the last step. Perhaps the tide rolled in, perhaps the shoe-buckle wing carried me there, but somehow, I found myself standing at the shoreline. Waves lapped at my toes, and I shivered—but the warmth seeping out my heart and through my veins stamped out the cold. The snorkel somehow made its way to my face, though I only vaguely recalled putting it on.

The moon peeked out from its hiding place and illuminated the tip of Inis Eala, scarlet berries from the hawthorn barely visible. I felt close. Closer than I'd ever felt before, and my heart did one of Darcy's jigs in my chest.

I held my breath. I closed my eyes. I dove.

Swish, into the water I went. I opened my eyes, gulping air in through my snorkel. Moonlight filtered through the blue-green water and a few out-of-bed minnows skirted by. The iciness of the ocean settled into my bones. But, as I glided smoothly through the water, I decided I was glad I hadn't worn my sweater or my big boots; better cold than drowned.

And so I flippered my feet through the water, bobbing up every now and then to make sure I was still headed for Inis Eala. The rest of the time, though, I kept my eyes shut and my ears open. I listened for wing-flapping, and I listened for swan-honking, but all I heard was my heart. *Take me there*, was what it said, and it drummed out those words again, again, again, as I swam across the blue-green sea, *thra-thump, thra-thump, thra-thump* . . .

Chapter 10

THE WATER WAS CALM, but the moon lost its bright. My limbs had long gone numb, but my feet kept kicking as if someone had flicked a switch in me to autopilot. When I bobbed up to check how close I was to Inis Eala, though, a shiver zipped down my spine. The air smelled of chalk dripping down sidewalks and witches' brew (which was what Nuala called hot cabbage soup) simmering on the stovetop and rubber umbrellas taken along "just in case." It smelled of wet sheep and dry blankets and cold hands and hot fires.

And then came a drop. Just one, teensy, innocent raindrop.

I had to get to shore. *Now.*

The thunder rolled in like a warhorse, at first a far-off trot soon blooming to a rollicking gallop, unstoppable and unbeatable.

I kicked and doggy-paddled as fast as my tired muscles would allow. Inis Eala seemed a thousand times farther away to my legs than to my eyes. So big, so close, yet so out of reach. I gasped for air as water filled my snorkel, filling my mouth with salt water and seaweed.

The water surrounding me turned white, and I tried to let the towering swells lift me up and over, but instead I went through them. I coughed, spluttered, threw off my snorkel, and rubbed the salt from my eyes. Inis Eala was no longer in view—nothing was, but the water engulfing me.

I wriggled up to the surface, expecting to be rushed under again, but for one glorious moment, I wasn't. And then the song came, reverberating around my head, knocking down all the walls of fear that cornered me in, as if they were made of cardboard instead of concrete. I whispered, *"Álainn, álainn, álainn . . ."* That was how Nuala taught me to say "beautiful" in Irish, but I saved the word for special occasions, and, my oh my, it turned the sea salt in my mouth to marzipan. It was a swan song.

As I looked up, however, terror struck my bones. I did not see a swan, but a wave five times my size curling over me like a changeling would a baby cradle, fingers outstretched.

Crash.

The wave dragged me under. But this time, hard as I kicked, I couldn't reach the surface. I reached, lunged for air, but only sunk deeper and deeper. Slowly, I squinted open my eyes, salt water stinging.

I looked down. Instantly, my stomach lurched; I could see nothing but the deep blue drop. I felt suddenly as if I were skydiving, waiting for the parachute to open.

I looked up. The surface felt even farther away than Inis Eala.

I looked around. Bubbles swirled past me, shapes shifted in the distances, just shadows, perhaps a merrow, perhaps a selkie . . . No. *Someone was there.* Someone small. Drowning. He or she or it was drowning. Then reality struck me. *We* were drowning. Both of us.

I kicked and flapped toward the figure, but it remained just a shadow at the end of my vision, sinking deeper down. My head ached for air. My lungs felt the way an accordion might in the hands of a fearless musician. Then, as if time stood still, the figure looked at me. I couldn't see its eyes, but I *knew* it looked at me. It was a girl, I could tell now by the dark hair ballooning around her.

I waved.

The figure gave a lazy wave back, and then, gently, seemed to fall asleep, as if the water were her deathbed.

"*No!*" I tried to shout, but a bubble trapped my voice.

I kicked harder toward her, but my muscles were failing now. She was too far away. I was too far away. I couldn't save her, and she couldn't save me; one of us was going to die, if not both.

It was just as that horrible thought snaked its way into my brain that something magical happened. A whirl of bubbles plunged through the surface toward the figure. I could tell it was an animal, a large animal at that. I considered dolphin at first, but there was something about it that was simply not fishlike. The bubbles rose, and then I saw: *wings*.

And I knew.

This was the swan. The same swan that rescued me that very morning, the same swan leading me to Inis

Eala. Whether Fiachra, Conn, or Ena, I knew not, but one thing was for sure: This swan was a child of Lir.

With a swish of its wing, it swept up the girl, pulling her higher, higher until, at last, they broke the surface. *She's saved,* I thought. And I half waited for the swan to come for me too, but it didn't. Dark spots blinked about my vision, and the pressure lifted from my chest. The water grew more comfortable, almost mattresslike. My eyes closed on their own accord. Something soft brushed my arm, and then death took me by the hand and hummed his sweetest lullaby.

Chapter 11

THE SOUND OF SCRAPING ROCKS—that was what awoke me. Light filtered through my eyelids, and I had the oddest feeling that I was not lying in my bed under Nuala's quilt. I was lying on wood. Grimy, splintery wood. I opened my eyes a crack. The sky stared down, rosy-cheeked but indigo-eyelashed, caught in an in-between hour of dark and light, dreaming and awake.

"Finnuala." The word slipped out like a rabbit from a magician's hat. At first, I didn't know what it meant—but then, ah yes, that would be my name. But who had said it?

I tried to heave myself up, but felt as if a pile of bricks were lying on my chest. I squeezed shut my eyes with the pain, and a hand landed on my shoulder, easing me back down to the scratchy wood.

"Where am I?" The groggy, dry-lipped words stumbled out my mouth.

"Lie down. Do not speak," said the voice again; it was quite clear that this was not a suggestion.

"Yeah, okay . . . ," I murmured. But then my eyes snapped open and I shot upright—or, at least I tried to, but only managed to lift myself two inches above the wood before collapsing back down. I knew that voice—strong and soft rolled into one. "*Nu—*"

"Hush. You'll strain your lungs."

A splash of a foot hitting shallow water sounded as Nuala hopped out of the rowboat and towed it to shore. Then a blurry face appeared in my vision. Nuala's hair was down in long, tumbling silver waves—a rare spectacle indeed, as most mornings Nuala tied it in a bun before the sparrows even started singing. Her skin was pallid and her lips quivered with a chill. Big dark circles brooded beneath her eyes, the kind that looked like thunderstorm clouds, and then I remembered. The storm.

"Now, lass," she said, extending a hand down to me, "up you go." She tugged, and I pulled, and slowly, with a

crackle of Nuala's back, we both stood. "That's it, now."
She led me out of the rowboat, and I wobbled onto the
sand.

My knees buckled and I braced myself for the ground,
but Nuala caught me by the armpits and steadily led me
across the beach. "You disobeyed me, Finn," she said as
we walked.

"I'm—"

"Your lungs, Finn. Do not speak."

I nodded, and Nuala continued. "I told you about the
waters. I warned you about the waves. That sea is as much
a graveyard as it is a playground. You promised me—"
Her voice chipped off there, and we were left with only
the sound of the water kissing the sand. And then she
whispered, "You always keep your word."

I wanted to drag all the sadness out of Nuala's voice,
wad it up in my pockets like old handkerchiefs. But I
couldn't. All I could do was follow her silently across the
beach. Nuala didn't ask much of me. She asked me to do
my schoolwork and feed the hens, stay clear of faery rings
and keep my room smelling more on the side of fresh
linens than curdled milk, but that was pretty much it—
that, and staying away from the ocean. And I betrayed her.

At the edge of the beach, Nuala found a rocky stair-case. Ivy and moss crawled the stone walls encircling the water. Mushrooms popped up in the cracks in the stone, and strange black berries dappled curling vines. Nuala helped me up each step, one foot at a time, the way I often helped her when we climbed the steeper cliffs of Donegal.

The island, I came to realize, felt much less friendly up close than far away, and thrice I lost my footing on the steps. Nuala, though, seemed to know every nook and cranny of the rock by heart, and she nimbly guided me up the staircase.

"Watch yourself here, lass," she said as I was just about to step in an ankle-sized crevice. "Don't want a broken foot, do we?" She eased me over the crevice and onto a grassy platform. Dew seeped between my toes as I gazed to the dusty pink horizon. As I looked to my left, I nearly tumbled back again, as not five paces to the left stood a house—a small one, albeit, with holes dotting the thatch roof and ivy seeping out from every crack in the stone, but a house it was.

I recognized it. It was the same house I had looked upon so many times before, the stark-white ramshackle cottage hardly a dot in the distance, now was a thousand times more real.

"Now," said Nuala, "let's get you inside."

I gaped at her. "Ins—"

"*Lungs*, Finn. I will tell you when to speak. Understand?"

The word *yes* nearly escaped my throat, but when Nuala tipped up her chin, I bit my tongue and swallowed the word. What I *really* wanted to know, though, was, what sort of person would live on wild Inis Eala, why Nuala and I were sneaking into this stranger's house, and how Nuala knew it was here to begin with.

But when Nuala pulled a key from a flowerpot I hadn't even seen (it was covered in a thick blanket of moss) and chinked it into the doorknob, I was positive something was up; what that something was, that was the mystery.

Nuala ushered me into the low-ceilinged cottage. She quickly closed the door behind us—only to have it slam to the ground, hinges cracking free from the doorframe.

"Well," muttered Nuala as light poured in. "There goes that door," and she proceeded to rummage around in a drawer of a wooden desk as if she owned it. As my eyes adjusted to the dark, I could see that the cottage was more of a workshop with a rusty-framed bed stuck in the corner. Dusty bottles and silver trinkets cluttered the wall shelves. Book piles rose like stalagmites from the floor, balancing unwashed teacups and half-melted candles. There was a peculiar scent of forest trees and mothballs to the house, and as I flopped down onto the bed, a sour-then-sweet aroma erupted into the air; it left a taste in my mouth like the lemon drops Da brought from Belfast.

"That's it now, good girl," said Nuala, still rattling about in the desk drawers. "But don't lie down just yet. There's a remedy *somewhere* in here—ah, here we are." Nuala twirled around to reveal a thimble-sized vial, its contents obscured by the thick dust coating its glass. "Drink," she instructed, striding over to my bedside.

My eyes bulged at the look of the dusty vial.

"*Drink*, Finn. Have I ever led you astray?"

I shook my head no and took the vial. I squinched up my face ready for the foul taste and downed the medicine, only to realize a moment too late that it tasted of bubble gum.

"Now rest," said Nuala, pushing me onto the mattress and tucking a blanket around me. "When you wake, you may speak."

I didn't hesitate at that. It was as if my entire body had been yearning to sleep, but my brain never got the message, and asleep I fell. And while I slept, I dreamed of a bird with wings made out of shoe buckles and a sea with waves made out of bones.

I AWOKE TO SUNLIGHT streaming through my eyelids. As my eyes flickered open, the dizzying sensation of waking in someone else's house hit my stomach, but disappeared as memory settled in. I was alone, but not for long. Nuala peeked around the fallen door, a basket in her arms.

"Ah, good, you're awake," she said, hurrying over to my bedside. "Do your lungs feel better?"

I nodded, realizing the pressure on my chest had lifted.

Nuala handed me a pile of blackberries from her basket and said, "Eat. If you like, you may speak now." She paused and added, "But I want the first thing out of that mouth to be an explanation of why you disobeyed me."

I was about to babble on about how I wasn't thinking, how it was a mistake, but . . . it *wasn't* a mistake. And I *had* thought about it. Nuala's words from the previous day rang in my ear: *"You may go when you are needed there."*

"I didn't disobey you, though," I said. My voice sounded horribly froglike.

Nuala raised her eyebrows.

"Not really," I croaked. "Someone needs me here— *look.*" And from my jeans pocket, I pulled the hawthorn bark that had fallen out of my locket after Sojourn returned it to me, after the swan that saved me nicked it from my throat.

But when I looked to the bark, it was message-less. I flipped it to the other side, but it was just as blank. "No," I whispered. "The sea must have washed the message off. But—but I swear—yesterday it said, *'Meet me at the bleeding tree.'* And—and I got my locket back, too, after the swan took it. A boy, Sojourn, got it for me, and this note was in it, and I just knew that swan left it for me, Nuala. I knew it in my head and in my heart and in my bones. I knew that swan needed me to meet him or her at the hawthorn tree on this very isle. Won't you believe me?"

Nuala pursed her lips, and I quickly added, "I am sorry, though. Really, truly sorry."

Nuala nodded and then breathed, "Why're you so keen on flyin' away, lass?"

"I . . ." My stomach flip-flopped. "I'm not."

"You got a father who loves you and a little girl who idolizes you and a town full of people who want to get to know you if only you'd let 'em. And you got me."

"I know," I said. "I *know*, I just . . ." The word *lonely* pounded in my heart, rattled my rib cage. "That's why, I guess. 'Cause I've got everythin', all these people who love me, and still I'm lonely. I'm always lonely and I don't know why. It's like a piece of me is missing, and it'd take a miracle to make me feel less alone.

"But if I could find the swans, if I could *find* them . . . maybe my miracle wouldn't feel so big. Maybe if I found them . . . my miracle'd feel more like somethin' I could ask for at Christmas or Easter. Small. Somethin' I could touch and hold, somethin' not too expensive or rare or hard to fit through the door. If I could find the swans, my miracle would feel like wishin' for a bag of lemon drops instead of a talking hippopotamus. That's why I want to fly," I said, my words finally slowing their rumble-tumble. "It en't about being here or there or anywhere. All I want is to give my dream a pair of wings."

I waited for Nuala to scold me for making excuses,

lined up my sorries in my mind. But she didn't. She just sat at the edge of my bed, closed-eyed, nodding. Finally, she said, "Maybe . . . maybe you should see the isle."

My heart sung a swan song and my eyebrows jumped three inches. "Really?" I gasped. "You mean it?"

Nuala waved a hand toward the door. "Come on. I want to show you that bleeding tree."

Chapter 12

WE CROSSED INIS EALA the way explorers would a new country. I knew I shouldn't call the isle my property, so instead, I decided I would be property of the isle. No place I'd stepped had ever felt so right and so wrong. It was, after all, the place the Children of Lir had taken their last humanly steps. But it was also the place where their littlest sister was saved. It was a place of tragedy and of hope, and whether the tale was real or not, every stone and twig and blade of grass pulsed with story.

Brambles of blackberries, bushes of hydrangea—blushed fairy-tale pinks and blues—and stone walls created a maze within the isle. The trickle of water leading to a larger waterfall rushed in my ears, and the hummingbirds sang.

When the ground grew scattered with wrinkled crimson berries, I knew we were getting close. And sure enough, one hill later, a tree rose on the horizon. It was attached to the side of a cliff, roots like octopus arms gripping the cliff. The wood twisted up like a swirl of whipped cream, and the trunk curled over the way Willow Oliver did, as if it were listening. Except the hawthorn looked more like it was listening *for* something, not *to* someone like Oliver. That was because its branches stretched out toward the sea, fingers permanently frozen in a wind-blown, west-facing arch, as if the tree yearned to touch America. As if it were waiting for a tree in Boston to reach out and grab its branches, pull it across the sea the way Nuala used to pull me over rain puddles.

"This tree is always in bloom," said Nuala as we drew closer.

"So you *have* been here before."

Nuala nodded. "Long ago."

The waves thrashing against the rock grew louder. I squinted, trying to make out the Slieve League Cliffs, where I had stood gazing out to this very spot not twenty-four hours ago, but all the cliffs on Donegal looked the same.

When we came close as we could to the tree, Nuala reached up to the tree's branches and picked off a handful of white flowers. She cupped my hands around them and said, "That hawthorn has a daughter halfway 'cross the world, Finn." Nuala's voice grew soft and soothing like fresh water over river rocks. That was how I knew I was in for a story.

"When I was a girl," Nuala said, "I lived here on this isle. It wasn't so deserted back then, but when business got low and money got tight, all of us scattered off to Dublin or London or Philadelphia or heaven knows where. Well, when my father decided to ship us off to America, I decided to take a piece of Inis Eala with me.

"I plucked a seed from this tree and stuffed my pockets with its flowers. Three weeks later, we ended up in a little mountain town called Starlight Valley in Virginia—that's a state over in America. My father promised there would be a better life for me there, but all I felt was lonely. So one day, I walked to the edge of the valley and planted my seed. I took the flowers from my pocket and played a game with the petals. This is how it went."

Nuala took a flower from my palm and plucked a petal. "I won't be lonely," she whispered, and the petal drifted off to the sea. "I will be lonely." She plucked another petal; it followed the first down the cliff. "I won't be lonely." She plucked another. And another. "I will be lonely." And on the last petal, she smiled. "I won't be lonely." She twirled the stem in her pinch before pocketing it in her patchwork-pocket jeans. "Except I would do it with a bunch of hawthorn flowers, and not all of 'em had five petals, mind you—that way I'd never know what fate I was gonna end up with.

"Well, magic must have worked in those petals, because that May, I met the most wonderful friends of my life. Their names were Margaret, Ed, and Oliver, and, my, did we have a good craic that summer."

"Wait—*Grandpa* Oliver?" I said.

"The very same." Nuala paused and eyed my hands. "Why don't you give those flowers a try. I've got a good feeling about them."

Ordinarily I would have shied away, except the flowers were already in my hands and Nuala's story had already crawled into my heart and I didn't really have anything to lose, so I whispered, "Okay."

I counted off each petal of each flower, breathing story words beneath my breath, "*I will be lonely. I won't be. I will be lonely. I won't be.*" And when I came to the final three petals, my heart sank. The first would be lonely. The second would be not lonely. And then I'd be stuck with *lonely, lonely, lonely.*

But as I tore off the first petal, something *magical* happened: The second petal pulled off too. I stared at the final petal, twirled it 'round the stem like a pony flying 'round a carousel. The words *won't be* fell from my mouth half by accident. By another accident, my lips slipped into a crooked moon smile.

Nuala's eyes sparked with galaxies drunk on stars and cleverness. She stared at my petal and breathed, "That's the sort of thing miracles are made of."

I kept smiling, but there was something about that word *miracles* that left a bitter taste in my mouth. It was flouncy and far-fetched, strung of pipe dreams and mythology. It was practically the same as *impossible*. So instead of miracles, I'd call it serendipity. That meant "happy mistake," and there's nothing impossible about a happy mistake. In fact, I realized, there was nothing more *possible* than a happy mistake.

I'd remember this petal. I'd keep it in my locket, soon as I got it back from Darcy, those three children in the photograph keeping it safe for me.

Recognition shivered my bones. "Nuala—the children in the locket—those were Oliver, Ed, and Margaret, weren't they? Your friends. And that tree they're sittin' in—that's the one you planted, en't it?"

Nuala paused, then said, "Indeed it is."

I beamed. I had names now, and that made them feel close. And later, I'd study their smiles and memorize their eyes and learn their stories too.

"Don't you still talk with 'em?"

Nuala bit her lip. "Afraid I've lost contact. Anyway. Here," said Nuala, pulling something shiny from a kitten-patterned pocket. "They're missin' you," and she handed me the locket.

The metal was warm to the touch, but nothing compared to the heat striking my forehead, sending sweat down my brow. "Where did you get that from?" I choked.

Nuala narrowed her eyes. "The beach, of course. That's how I knew you'd tried to swim here. Found it along with your field journal and didn't want it getting swept out with the tide."

"But Nuala," I said, "I didn't have the locket tonight. Darcy did."

Chapter 13

I'D NEVER SEEN NUALA'S ARMS move so fast as she rowed the little boat back across the sea. When we came upon the shore, we were greeted with wailing. A woman was sitting in the sand, head between her knees, breath spiked with cries. It was Nanny Hurley. Darcy's dance teacher, Miss Eileen, sat beside her, arm wrapped over Miss Hurley's shoulder. Sean and Mary, Darcy's teenage neighbors, were holding each other tight. Every teacher and student from the village school was there, some crying, some holding their head in their hands. Mr. McCann paced back and forth along the beach, puffy-eyed, as two policemen surveyed the area, clipboards in hands. It seemed the only person missing was Da.

My throat tightened, heart thumped thrice as fast. When the police caught sight of Nuala and me rolling onto the beach, they hurried over to us.

"Where is she—the child; have you found her yet?" Nuala babbled. I'd never heard Nuala *babble* before.

"If we'd found 'em, we wouldn't still be looking for 'em," said the first policeman, scowling down at us. "Names, please."

Before either me or Nuala could answer, my teacher, Mrs. Flanagan, and the village librarian, Mrs. Dempsey, tackle-hugged me from the side. Mrs. Flanagan planted a kiss on my forehead and Mrs. Dempsey squeezed my cheeks till they burned. "You're *safe*, thank the good and gracious Lord, you're *safe*," bubbled Mrs. Flanagan.

The policeman tilted up his chin. "I take it this is the elder missing child? Finnuala O'Dálaigh-Sé?"

Mrs. Flanagan and Mrs. Dempsey both nodded vigorously as the villagers gathered 'round me. I passed around hugs like Mr. McCann would Guinness, but the policeman soon shooed them off. "Now . . . tell me where you're coming in from, why don't you?"

"Inis Eala," said Nuala, nodding to the isle, and she told all that had happened that morning.

When Nuala finished, the policeman said, "And why were *you* at Inis Eala?"

A flicker of discomposure crossed Nuala's eyes, but she recovered within seconds. "I'm not sure what you mean, Officer," she said.

"Well, if you didn't know your granddaughter was stuck at sea, what prompted you to go to the isle? You fancy boat rides in thunderstorms?"

I turned to Nuala, wanting to ask, *Yes, why* were *you rowing to Inis Eala?* But Nuala gave me a look that said I'd better hold my tongue.

"I do actually," she said.

The policeman raised his eyebrows.

"My father was a fisherman. Took me out to sea during storms when I was a lass. I go out every now and then and think of him."

I could tell she was lying—or, at least, not telling the whole truth.

The policeman jotted down Nuala's answer on his clipboard, then turned to me. "Now, tell me something, child. Marjorie Hurley says you slept over at the Brannons' house last night, but left sometime between ten o'clock at night and eight in the morning, when she found you and Darcy gone. So my question is, who left first—you or the Brannon girl?"

"Me," I said. "I left just after Darcy fell asleep. I know nothing, I swear it. If I had any inf—"

"I trust them, Officer," piped Miss Hurley. "Finn and Nuala wouldn't hurt a fly."

"Just standard procedure, miss," said the policeman. "Now, does this paper mean anything to you?" He held up a scrap of sparkly pink paper that read:

Finn:
Gone to find the swans.
Be back by morning.
—Darcy

My arms prickled with goose bumps. I felt light-headed, but managed to spit out, "No."

The policeman nodded, scribbled something on his clipboard, then said, "I'm sorry for your loss," as if she were certainly dead.

The world spun, colors smashed into colors, blurring into sickly browns and greens. The image of the drowning girl and the swan floated through my mind. Somewhere far away, I heard Nuala say, "C'mon," and she led me through the crowd and up the stone staircase.

Da's little blue punch buggy was parked at the top of the cliff, but Da wasn't inside. We clambered in and drove away. I didn't feel the summer-sunned leather burning my skin. I didn't hear the radio music Nuala played. I didn't see the willows flying by outside the window. Gray was the world without Darcy, and it was my fault. *My fault, my fault, my fault.* I wished I'd never told her that stupid story. I wished I'd never even heard it.

When we pulled into the drive, the cottage door swung open. In the threshold stood a man, jaw clenched and fists tight. His face was scarlet and his hair fluffed up in a mess as if he'd been running his fingers through it all week. Fear shivered through me, but then I realized . . . it was Da. Just Da.

Not once had I seen him so furious. I cracked open the car door and tiptoed out, shielding my eyes with a strand of hair. But when I peeked out from the white-blond, Da was stomping toward me. "How dare you," he spat.

I felt myself shrinking away against the blue Volkswagen as Da fired, "I trusted you, Finn. I trusted you to be responsible, spend the night at Darcy's, and come trotting right on home. I guess I don't know you well as I thought I did."

That last part cut me like a knife made of ice. I could deal with Da being angry with me. I could deal with him feeling disappointed or frustrated. But there was something about those words that made me afraid Da might disappear. *I don't know you well as I thought I did.* Like we were on the edge of becoming strangers.

"Lorcan—" tried Nuala, but Da wouldn't listen.

"So how does this make me look, Finn?" he continued. "Stupid! That's how."

"Lorcan, please—"

"I can't even *look* at you right now. Go to your room."

For the first time that day, tears spilled from my eyes. I knew I had betrayed Nuala, but not once had I considered I was betraying Da too. So I went. I ran into the house and up to my room, and I cried into Nuala's quilt until my nose stuffed up and my eyes went dry.

And by the time I came back down, the dishes were done and the floor was swept and the house mouse was nibbling the sweet-and-sour lemon drops from the bag. Da's suitcase was gone and so was his punch buggy. He'd left the door half open and two mice scurried in to join the third. By the time I turned for the stairs, the lemon drops were gone too.

Chapter 14

"I want to get your lungs checked by a doctor."

Breakfast had been silent up until that point. Neither me nor Nuala had mentioned Da or Darcy since the previous day.

I chased a sausage around my plate with my fork. "I'm *fine*, Nuala," I said. "I haven't been to a doctor in—"

"You don't spend six minutes underwater and *not* get checked by a doctor, Finn. I've already phoned Mrs. Flanagan and told her you won't be in school today. Besides that, the hospital's got your appointment all set up."

"Right, fine," I muttered. I stood to grab my sweater, but then turned back. "The *hospital*? Why don't I just see Dr. Clarke?"

"Dr. Clarke is sick with a bout of bronchitis today," explained Nuala.

"The *doctor* is sick?"

Nuala nodded. "It happens, lass, and the hospital was kind enough to set you up with an expert pulmonologist."

"A *pulmonologist?*"

"Now, it's a two-hour trip into Belfast, so I suggest you bring something to occupy yourself."

"Fine," I said again, but I didn't like it one bit. I didn't like this business-as-usual thing, not when two of the people I cared most about were gone. But I didn't have the energy for an argument, so I stood, grabbed my sweater and sneakers, and headed out the door.

I SLEPT MOST OF THE TAXI ride to Belfast, but when I woke, I knew we had arrived by the greyman. The greyman was a faery of sly tricks and stealth. He brought the fog and the rain and the smoke, and he brought the sad and the loss too. He pushed down strangers' heads, so all they did was stare at the sidewalk on their way to work. He slunk 'round children's ankles, grayed out their vision, so they got lost on their way to school. He snuck those *just*

one more cigarettes into soldiers' pockets and dragged eyelids down, breathing *tired* down unsuspecting necks.

Today, the greyman was out in full force, blanketing the tops of buildings. When I stepped out of the cab, he sent a chill down my spine. I covered my nose; the air reeked of burning rubber and gunpowder.

Nuala and I exchanged glances as the taxi sped off into the fog. Nuala tried to smile, but I could tell the greyman was working on her too. She managed to contort her mouth into a half grin and breathed, "Why—why, what a surprise; Niall's is open again. Perhaps we'll share an ice cream after the appointment, what d'you think, Finn?"

But as we strode past Niall's Country Creamery, I saw that the lights in the window Nuala had seen were not real lights at all. They were reflections of a fire licking at a pile of old car tires on the side of the street. The ice cream shop was already covered in graffiti, though it had been open just three months ago. The green paint read:

Ready to Fight.
—IRA

That was the army Da fought for—the Irish Republican Army.

The streets were filled with noise, but no one seemed to talk. Cars honked, sirens blared. British soldiers lined the streets, half of them standing post at buildings, never looking anyone in the eye. The other half leaned slack against crumbling walls and smoked cigarettes. Many of them were just boys, hardly older than me. I knew I wasn't supposed to like them, and I didn't, but I couldn't bring myself to hate them the way Da did.

"Two more blocks, lass, keep up," said Nuala, and I realized I had been staring at one soldier slouched against a soot-stained bakery.

"Nuala?"

"What, lass?" She looped her arm through mine and held on tight.

"Why don't we like 'em?"

"Who?"

"The soldiers."

"The British ones?"

I nodded.

"'Cause they're takin' our land, that's why."

"But you always say land belongs to no one 'cept the faery."

Nuala's lips blanched. "You'll understand when you're older."

"But—"

"Don't talk of things you know nothing about, Finn."

I stopped in my tracks and glared up at Nuala. "Why do you do that?"

"Do *what*, Finn?" she huffed, glancing furtively to a soldier brushing past us.

"Act like I'm not old 'nough for anythin'. Like I can't think for myself or—or make my own decisions—"

Nuala ran her fingers through her hair and muttered, "I should've called the doctor in Dublin."

A couple shouts echoed from around the corner, so I raised my voice. "I en't a little girl anymore!"

"Well, you certainly *act* like it, running off to find those swans, good *Lord*. We wouldn't even be here if it weren't for your foolishness. You simply don't listen to me."

The shouts grew louder, so Nuala and I backed under a tattered awning, as if that would block out the noise.

"Foolishness? Ha! You know what? I know you made up that story 'bout your da being a fisherman and going out in storms in his memory. I know you went out to see the swans. I know you wanted to see 'em just as much as I did. If there's anyone foolish here, it's you—you went out for no reason at all, other than to see the swans like some tourist watchin' the solstice at Newgrange. But me? Those swans *mean* something to me. They mean everything to me, and there en't nothin' foolish about what I want. There en't nothin' childish about it neither."

Nuala's lips pursed. She knew I was right but was just too stubborn to say so. "What *do* you want, Finn?" she finally said. Her voice then lowered. "I know you're lonely. But there are other ways to fill a hole in your heart."

"I want a family, Nuala!" I burst. "A *real* family."

Nuala's eyes fell.

"I—I didn't mean that." I stumbled back.

There was something off about Nuala's face: Her wrinkles were sparkling. I considered for a moment that it was faery dust sprinkled by the greyman perhaps, but no. Those were tears. Slender, shimmery tears trickling down the valleys of her face. It occurred to me that I had never seen Nuala cry. I didn't like it. I didn't like it one bit.

I tore my gaze from Nuala's face and took off into the streets. I had to get *away, away, away*. Away from Nuala and away from Da and away from Darcy. Away from Belfast and away from Donegal and away, away, away from that Inis Eala. I hardly noticed the hollering growing louder around me, faster, harsher, colder—

But then the gunshot came.

Chapter 15

THE FIRST SHOT silenced the shouts.

The second started them up again. Only this time, the shouts mingled with a scream of agony and a dozen screams of terror.

I stood frozen. Fire blazed. Street children scattered. A beggar dropped his can of coins and fled. Three soldiers barreled past me. My heart beat hummingbird fast.

Someone called my name.

Someone called my name.

Someone called my name.

I turned. Nuala was racing toward me, arm outstretched. *Grab her hand*, my head shouted, but my arm didn't get the message.

Nuala's voice rang out: *"Finn! Finn, get back h—"*

A third shot.

I crouched to the ground, clamped my hands over my ears. My mouth tasted like ash.

A body tumbled down on me. Something wet trickled through my hair. I crawled out from under the body and squinted through the fog. A splotch of red bloomed like a rose on the body's patchwork sweater. Rubble dusted her silver hair, gripped like stickers to the tears still glistening in her wrinkles.

"No," I breathed. But then my heart tugged my vocal cords like a bellman before church, and I screamed louder than any gunshot. "Nuala? Nuala, what's going on? Tell me what's wrong. Tell me what's *wrong.*" I lunged for her, scraping my knees along the ground, and began to shake her.

And then my heart stopped for a moment. "No . . . she's not dead. SHE'S NOT DEAD!" I grabbed her head, heavy as Connemara marble, and I held Nuala against my chest, feeling her mouth for hot breath. None came.

A man with a gun—British or Irish, I couldn't tell— turned to me and shouted, "Get out of here, kid! Someone get that kid out!"

A pair of hands seized my armpits and began to drag me away from Nuala.

"STOP!" I screeched as her head slipped from my fingers. "Get *off* me! That's my grandmother!"

I scraped at the asphalt with my fingernails, but the hands did not let loose. They dropped me by a dump truck three blocks away, then wiped off the blood on my jeans. The hands' owner whispered something in my ear, and though I could tell he spoke English, his words sounded a different language. He stood after that and flew off down the street. I watched him disappear into the mouth of the greyman, and then I watched the greyman descend on me. His lips opened wide and dark, and he swallowed me too, hungry as war's dear friend, death.

SOMETHING WAS BEEPING. And blinking. Feet shuffled, whispers fluttered. "She's waking up!"

"No, she en't."

"Look at the *monitor*."

"Just family for now, please."

More shuffling. The click of a door closing.

My eyes flickered open, and I suddenly felt as if

someone were continuously dropping bricks on my head. A white room blurred into view, and a woman dressed in white fiddled with a tube stuck in my arm. A man leaned over me, eyes swollen and nose red, scar above his lip.

"Da?" My voice crackled on the word. Over his shoulder I saw three faces peeping through the door's window—Mrs. Flanagan, Miss Hurley, and Mr. McCann. "Where—"

Da nodded and took my hand in his, calloused and warm. "*Shh*. It's me, baby girl."

I tried to prop myself up on the pillows behind me, but Da pushed me back down. "Where's Nuala?"

Da's mouth twitched. "She's . . ." The veins in his neck clenched tight.

He didn't need to finish. Everything came flooding back: the shouts, the crowds, the gunshots, the fall . . . I lunged for Da's neck, pulling him into a hug. *"I'm sorry,"* I said. And I said it again and again and again until my throat grew scratchy, all the while Da cooing, "It en't your fault, Finn." But he didn't know a thing. It *was* my fault. It was my fault because Nuala was right about everything—I'd been stupid to go to the isle. If I hadn't gone, I wouldn't have had to come to Belfast. And if we hadn't come to Belfast, Nuala wouldn't be . . .

I wept on Da's shoulder while he cautiously stroked my back as if he'd forgotten how to comfort. Maybe he'd never learned in the first place; it didn't matter. Nuala was gone. *Gone, gone, gone.* That was all that mattered, and the word pulsed in my mind like a story I didn't want to hear. *Gone, gone, gone.* Except for her stories. I had never wanted so much for her stories not to belong to me.

THE HOSPITAL LET ME GO later that day, and Da carried me out to the little blue punch buggy. "You're gettin' big for this," he said as he heaved me onto the back seat under one of Nuala's patchwork blankets. "Not such a baby girl anymore, I s'pose."

I supposed not. Maybe yesterday or the day before, but not today. Today I felt a hundred years old.

Da drove so fast out of Belfast, you'd think the place was burning—I supposed it was. He stopped once in Derry to pick up a black dress at a secondhand store, then drove on. The whole drive, the only words we exchanged were these:

"Awfully quiet back there."

"Yes."

A hollowness took hold of my stomach, ripping from it every happy memory of Nuala and me, dyeing them the color sadness.

Another hour, and we pulled up to the drive of the little cottage half-in-half-out of the willow glades. It was just as we left it. The sheep were grazing in the garden. The jeans were hanging on the line. The doormat was flipped up at the corner.

I undid my seat belt and reached for the door handle, but before I could turn it, Da piped, "Finn—" Da's voice cracked on my name. "You're leaving tomorrow. I'm sorry, baby girl."

I felt light-headed, so I leaned back into the seat. "Wh-what d'you mean?"

Da craned his neck over the front seat and looked me sadly in the eye. "You're gonna go to America for a while, Finn. You'll pack your things tonight. Flight leaves in the mornin'."

"America?" I breathed. "What are you talking about? I can't go to America!"

Da nodded. "Just for a little while. Two, three weeks tops, until I figure out a plan."

"But—but—where will I live—who—America? I've got to look for Darcy if they haven't found her yet. And . . .

America? Why can't I just live with you in Belfast? And Nuala—what about her funeral? What's the dress for if I haven't got a funeral to wear it to?"

Da curled back to his seat so I couldn't see his face. "The police are doing everything they can to find Darcy. And you can't live in Belfast with me because, well, because it clearly en't safe. 'Sides, you, Finn? You in Belfast? You need the mountains and the trees and the lakes and the sea. You're a ramblin' girl. The city en't meant for ramblin' girls."

He spoke as if it were about me, but I knew the truth. It was about him, how he was too busy to care for me. I wanted to tell him that he was a rambler too, that he came and left and hopped around from home to Belfast to Dublin to Cork and back to Belfast. Wherever the army put him, he went. And then I wanted to tell him that we didn't have to be ramblers, that we could settle down together. I could live without the mountains, and he could live without the city lights, perhaps find a happy medium somewhere. I would even live in Belfast if it meant being with Da. But no, he wouldn't have that. I was too much a bother.

"And about Nuala," continued Da. "She will be cremated, and we'll have a ceremony for her when you return."

"When I *return*? No, it's got to be now."

Da ignored me. "While in America, you'll live with your mother in Starlight Valley, Virginia."

My stomach dropped. "My *mother*?"

"Yes, your mother—"

"But—but Ma's in a grave. I've seen it with my own two eyes: *Aobh Róisín O'Dálaigh-Sé, May She Rest in Peace,* is what it says. And wait, Starlight Valley—that's where Nuala lived when she was a girl!"

Da sighed. "One thing at a time, Finn. First thing's first . . ." He sighed again as if the words clung to his throat like molasses. "Aobh, she en't your ma. She would've loved you if she'd known you, baby girl, but she en't your ma."

"You're telling me I have a mother—a live one, I mean." My body didn't seem to know what to do with itself—the hair on my arms stood up and my stomach flopped and my feet prickled with pins and needles.

"Her name is Aoife."

When I was little, I would search for traces of Ma in the attic. There weren't pictures of her. Da said she wasn't sentimental. But he did have her voice. Just a scrap of it. A record he played for me called *Aobh and Me, Christmas 1945*. I never figured out who *me* was, because the second voice in it was female, so it sure couldn't have been Da, and it sounded nothing like Nuala. Sometimes, when Da was home long enough, I'd hear him playing the tape in his room, over and over again. And I'd lean in close and listen too. But now I knew that hadn't really been my mother. That woman hadn't even known me.

"Aoife," I repeated, hollow voiced. The name struck my heart with memories of nightmares I used to have about the horrible mother in "The Children of Lir." It nearly sounded like *Aobh*, but had more flounce to it and was a fraction as pretty. Even with a name like *Aoife*, though, the word *mother* skipped around my mind like fireworks because that was a word I would have to get used to using more often. It gleamed of new and shiny treasures.

"She en't all that bad, Finn. We had our disagreements, but she en't that bad. An' if one thing's for sure, it's that she loved you."

"She loved me?" Questions whipped fast through my

head. "If she loved me so much, why'd she leave me? Why'd she leave and never come back?"

"Because . . . I don't know."

"And why'd you keep her a secret from me? Why'd you pretend Aobh was my mother when she wasn't? And why—"

Da twisted 'round to face me again and pleaded, "Finn! Just give her a chance for me, all right? You'll be home in no time anyway. I promise that. Okay?"

"Da?"

"Hmm?"

I pulled a thread from the collar of the funeral dress Da had shoved in the back seat. I wanted to confess to him what I'd said to Nuala just before she died, and I wanted to tell him that I didn't mean it. That no family would ever compare to the family I had with him and Nuala, that even though our family was different, it was perfect. I wanted to tell him that when he left us the other night, my heart nearly burst with loneliness. I wanted to tell him how the emptier my heart grew, the heavier it grew too, which didn't make any sense at all. Nothing made sense anymore, really.

All I knew was that all I had was Da. And some-where across the ocean, I had a mother. Somewhere, I had a family. Somewhere, I belonged. So instead, I said, "I'll go."

Da stretched over the front seat and pecked a kiss on my forehead. "That's my girl."

"Just one thing," I said. "Do I look like her?"

Da furrowed his eyebrows. "What?"

I nodded. "Do I look like her? My mother."

Da's jaw jumped thrice before he finally spat, "Not in the slightest."

Chapter 16

NUALA'S RATTY BROWN SUITCASE stared up at me. Empty.

My yellow duffel, I had left at Darcy's, and I had no intention of going back there. So, Da dug Nuala's suitcase out of her wardrobe because I had no intention of visiting Nuala's room either. Everything would be exactly where she left it. The bed might not be made, just waiting for her to come home to it, flop down, invite me in, and spin a bedtime story. Her hiking boots would be kicked against the wall, and she'd have a pile of laundry in the corner that still smelled of her rosemary soap.

I couldn't avoid everything, though, and that was because wherever I went, whatever I did, I expected her. I expected her out hanging clothes on the line, and I expected her at the stove cooking porridge, and whenever the door creaked open, I expected her big-footed steps in the hall. She was never there, of course. She would never be there.

I spent half the night clearing out my closet—I couldn't sleep. The other half, I wandered the stairs, up and down, up and down, up and down. Then I conquered the hallways, crisscross, crisscross, crisscross. Then I opened and closed the doors, *clickety-clack, clickety-clack, clickety-clack*. Then I stood.

I stood there for hours, my hand on the doorknob, and I *wished*. I wished doorknobs were like clay. That way, I would be able to feel the mold of Nuala's hand, just this once more. I would be able to feel her every wrinkle, every scar, every callus. I would hold tight her hand in my grasp . . . just this once more.

I left without a click, without a clack.

Chapter 17

By MORNING, I STOOD IN A VALLEY of jeans and board games, old math tests and cracked seashells. *Two weeks*, I thought. *What do I need for two weeks?*

"Finn!" Da called from downstairs. "Hurry up; it's time to go!"

Crumbs. I spun twice around before I spotted the black funeral dress strewn over my bedpost. I grabbed it and smoothed it flat on Nuala's quilt so I wouldn't forget about it when I came back.

I grabbed from the top of my sock drawer, my Sunday dress—a lace-hemmed seafoamy frill of a thing. I hated it, but wanted to look nice when I met my mother, so I tossed it into the suitcase.

I was about to grab a pair of socks too, but something more interesting caught my eye. From the left-hand corner of the drawer, I pulled out a small dollhouse full of all the hawthorn (and a few willow and ash) leaves I had collected with Nuala. *"Our orphanage of leaves,"* Nuala had called it once, because after we collected the leaves, we would name them and sew stories for them. *"We'll call this one Aisling,"* she'd said, *"because that means 'dream.' And this little leaf, she got blown all the way to Donegal through a faery bride's dream. And this one, here, we'll call Cian. He made it here tightrope walking on a raven's breath. Did you know that?"*

I felt silly, all of a sudden, having been busying myself with socks and sweaters, when all that mattered was Nuala. I tossed the dollhouse in, then snapped shut the suitcase.

My field journal lay spread open behind my door— Nuala must have tucked it there after coming home from Inis Eala. Feathers still stuck out of every page like over-eager bookmarks. I kicked it under my bed. I didn't want to think about those stupid swans ever again.

I gave my room a good long look before remembering one last thing: the hawthorn petal. I'd left it in the back of my patch-pocket jeans, but where? *Ah.* They sat wadded up behind the curtain. I clambered across a mound of T-shirts—

"Finn, come *on*!" called Da.

I shoved my hand into the left pocket and revealed the tiny petal, now a ghost of a thing, yellowed like old parchment. I unclasped my locket and gave the petal to Margaret to hold. She smiled up at me as always, but just before I clasped the locket shut, I could have sworn I saw her wink. I narrowed my eyes, studied the curl of her short hair and the way her flowery dress caught in the breeze. She was exactly the same as always, and so were Ed and Oliver. Trick of the light.

Da's footsteps pounded up the staircase.

I snapped shut the locket and stumbled toward my door, shouting, "Coming!"

On the way out, I snatched my high-tops, then hopped down the stairs, lugging the suitcase in one hand, and in the other, wrangling the sneakers onto my feet. Darcy's shoe-buckle wing was still looped around my ankle, and I tucked it into my sneaker to make sure it didn't fall off. I didn't want my last bit of Darcy to go missing too. I met Da halfway down the stairs, and he took my suitcase. "Packing light?"

"Don't need much."

Da nodded. "On our way, then?"

I crossed the kitchen, but as I neared the doorway, I stopped short. "The mice," I muttered.

"The what?" said Da.

I hurried over to the cabinet and pulled from the top shelf a bag of cheese puffs. I shook the puffs into three bowls and laid the bowls in the corner of the floor. "I won't have the mice starvin' to death while I'm gone," I told Da.

The look he gave me, I wanted to capture in a bottle because that look, that *look*, made me nearly laugh out loud. And laughing—even just near laughing—well, that was a feat that felt even more insurmountable than swimming to Inis Eala.

TWO AND A HALF HOURS LATER, Da and I stood at a glass window gazing out over Belfast. A red-white-and-blue-winged plane wheeled around a large pavement, sending butterflies down my throat. "That's it?" I said, looking up to Da.

Da checked his watch and nodded. "Imagine so."

"Right, then," I said. I tried to sound businesslike, but I couldn't keep the fear from my voice.

Da couldn't either, even as he said, "You'll be fine."

I clenched the muscles in my neck to keep the tears at bay. "Promise you'll write?"

"Promise," said Da. He kissed my head, his hair flopping onto my forehead, then added, "And when you get back, you and I are gonna have a *feast* of lemon drops."

I smiled. "Da?"

"Hmm?"

I stood on my tiptoes and swished aside Da's bangs with my fingernails. I wished he had let Nuala cut them one last time. She used to cut them for him—always too short for his taste—but they would grow back within a month. "Your hair is in your eyes."

Da smiled wryly at me. "What would you say to your old man growing it long like a hippie?"

I giggled and Da planted another kiss on my forehead. Then he stuffed his hands in his pockets and nodded toward the gate. "Go on, now. Don't want to miss it."

I nodded and headed for the gate. *I'll do them right this time*, I thought. *My goodbyes.* I'd do them the way I'd have done for Nuala if I'd known I'd never see her again. I looked back thrice to Da, waving each time. And when the plane took off, I blew a kiss to my Ireland, whispering *love you, love you, love you*, till the clouds became like ground, till the heather's lament became breeze in my ears.

PART II

America

Chapter 18

"TEN MINUTES UNTIL ARRIVAL; please prepare for land-ing," announced the pilot from a loudspeaker. He had an American accent, the kind where the vowels slanted and the consonants went slack, the kind that makes you taste iced tea and hear banjo music.

I opened my locket and twirled the hawthorn petal in my pinch, while the woman beside me snored, lolled over on my shoulder.

"It won't be so bad," I whispered to the boy in the photograph smiling at the camera—I supposed that must be Ed; Grandpa Oliver was camera shy, so I assumed he was the boy glancing away. "I'll get to meet her after all, my—" What should I call her? Mother? Ma? "Aoife," I decided. Aobh had been Ma for as long as I could remember. It would be too strange to call her anything but. "Though now that I think about it," I added (to Margaret, this time) as I rolled up the sleeves of the shirt I'd nervous-sweated through, "I wish I'd brought more clothes."

And then I turned to Oliver. "I wish I'd brought you too," I told him. And I thought about what Nuala had said about planting a hawthorn tree in Starlight Valley from a seed of Inis Eala's hawthorn, how it made her less lonely. I wished I'd taken a seed from Oliver's willow.

"Me?"

No. I knew that voice. I hated that voice. Something like lightning cracked my spine. I whipped around, my sleeping neighbor waking and surreptitiously wiping the drool from her chin. Sojourn sat in the row behind me, that spidery smirk playing at his mouth and clawing under my skin like nails on a chalkboard.

"Forgot about it, did you, love?" he said. "I think *someone* owes me for a plane ticket."

The deal with the locket, I remembered from the first

time I met Sojourn. I had promised to take him to America with me. "You followed me."

Sojourn shrugged. "At least one of us has got to keep their promises."

I thought of the nastiest word I knew and spat, "You're despicable."

"Thank you," he sneered.

"Have you no mercy?" I huffed. "Don't you know all I've been through? Don't you know why I'm even on this plane?"

Sojourn flapped his hand as if he were swatting away a fly. "Yeah, yeah, poor baby."

"Whatever," I said, turning back to my seat. I had to put up with him for another ten minutes before the plane landed, and then he'd be stuck who-knows-where in America and I'd never see him again. He'd blow through places the way he blew through Carroway, rile up some otherwise nice folks, and then be on his merry way. He didn't know where I was headed, and I wasn't about to tell him.

But then came the tap, a jabbing, bone-white finger on my shoulder accompanied by that insufferable voice. "Meet you in Starlight Valley."

THE TAXI CLATTERED DOWN dirt paths, over too-big rocks and loose-lying branches. The farther away from Lynchburg we drove, the narrower the roads twisted and the taller the mountains grew. Mist fogged the windows and pebbles flew up from the ground, clinking against the side of the car, causing the driver to grumble, "And this car's a new one too . . ."

I sat in the back seat, holding tight to my suitcase to keep it from hurling through the windshield. I had changed into my Sunday dress at the airport, but was deeply regretting it as I felt rather queasy with all the bumping. I tugged at the lace collar to give myself air and closed my eyes, pretending I was in a boat instead— I never got seasick—but was greeted only by the image of Nuala rowing us to shore away from Inis Eala. My stomach yanked even tighter.

When at last we came upon a wall of trees, we rolled to a stop. For the first time in many years, I could not decipher which type of tree they were—thick and gnarled, certainly conifer, but spiked with thorns, needle-long.

"Road stops here, kid," said the driver, squinting at

the address Da wrote for me on a slip of paper. "Starlight Valley's just beyond those trees. That'll be forty-two, fifty."

"But—I've no idea where to go, how to get in," I said.

The driver shrugged. "Beats me. Haven't driven into that place for years, ever since those trees popped up. They say no one comes, no one goes."

My stomach squirmed again. I was in the middle of nowhere with no way of finding my way into the valley without being stabbed to death by a forest of needle trees. *You couldn't have told me that before*, I wanted to tell the driver, but I held my tongue. I reached into my pocket for the money, and pulled out—*crumbs*—a handful of Irish pounds. I'd forgotten to exchange them into dollars at the airport.

"Any day now," pressed the driver.

I made a series of *er*s and *uh*s as the driver tapped his fingers on the steering wheel. I glanced furtively toward the window, wondering first how fast I could run—fast, but surely not faster than a taxi—and then how sharp those thorns really were. But then I saw it. A hole in the branches had appeared, and standing within it was a woman.

Impossible, I thought, for there wasn't a doubt in my mind that the trees had been thick as custard but a moment ago, not a branch or twig letting a droplet of light through.

Branches framed the woman like a photograph. She was tall and willowy, sleek as a selkie seal. Her skin stretched taut over her cheekbones, and her eyes glittered green as the thorn trees. She wore a white fur coat that draped across her shoulders, soft as snow, despite the hot summer sun, and on her tiny feet were a pair of dainty stilettos, heels carved from what appeared to be wood painted black and orange. Her hair was blond like mine, but hers was darker, the color of luxury and sophistication, like spun threads of gold. They fell around her face in curls like a 1940's movie star's. She looked *fancy*, the sort of person who served salt in little dishes and never got the hiccups.

I almost believed Da was right about me looking nothing like her—but then she smiled. Apple-lipped and dimpled cheeks, she looked like me. But there was someone else in her too. And I knew Nuala was Aobh's mother, not Aoife's, but still, there was something in the lines around Aoife's lips that whispered *Nuala*. It made my skin prickle. Tears stung my eyes at the very thought of Nuala.

Darling was the first thing out of her mouth. I couldn't hear her, of course, but the word was written on her lips.

I rolled down my window and stared as she glided over to the taxi.

From the front seat, the driver huffed, "Every minute you sit there, I add another twenty-five cents, you know."

When Aoife reached the window, she bent down and kissed my cheek. Her lips were cold, but soft. I said nothing. My eyes caught on her white coat. Up close, I realized it was not made of fur, but feathers. Hundreds and hundreds of swan feathers stitched together. Chills scurried about my spine.

"You must be Finnuala," she said. The lilt of her voice was something I had never heard before—not quite American, not quite Irish. It was a halfway voice.

My own voice caught in my throat. I meant to say "yes," or "hello," or "pleased to meet you." Instead, I spluttered, "Actually, they—er—call me Finn now."

Aoife peeked over to the driver and flashed a hundred-dollar bill. "Keep the change," she said, and opened the taxi door.

I stepped out of the cab, sneakers sinking into the moist soil as Aoife took my suitcase and slammed shut the door. She took my shoulder and squeezed me close, leading me to the gap in the wall of thorns. As we entered, Aoife whispered in my ear, "This is Starlight Valley."

I didn't know what I was expecting, but there was something about the place that made me wonder if there was such thing as a yellow greyman. Old greyman's little brother perhaps, little goldman. Blue misty mountains surrounded the place—beautiful, lovely—but caging. The valley was sunlit, but it swallowed me in a sadness I could not explain.

A small ravine cut between the thorn trees and the path, and we crossed a wooden bridge to the isle in the valley.

The path we came to was cloaked by alders and honeysuckle, though, as far as I could tell, the thorn trees seemed to ring around the valley—I could just make out the tip-tops of them on the other side. Up and over a hill, I could see a small village of shops and houses. A church steeple and a clock tower with its hands stuck at 7:32 rose above the hill, and there, in the far distance, something glinted. Something big and white and starry and bright. Something magical.

But the strangest thing of all was, I never heard the engine of the taxi revving up or the tires against the mountain stones as it sped away. And when I looked back to see if it was still sitting there, I saw nothing but thorn trees. The bridge and the gap, they just disappeared.

Chapter 19

I KNEW A STORY ABOUT A CHILD who followed a faery to an isle of clear waters and red berries. Both the faery and the child were obsessed with each other, and neither one could help from drawing close together. It happened in a dream, while the world was resting by the fire, weeping. The child took the faery's limp wrist, and they wandered into faeryland, hand in hand. What happened after that, I knew not, other than the child did not return. Some stories were just like that. Stopping in the middle of their paths, quick as gunshots—

Gunshots. Blood. Gone. I shook away the memories like shaking stray autumn leaves from my hair before they could squeeze my heart too tight.

I remembered the story as Aoife led me through the village built of sloping shops. Some held flopped-over menus and crackled pies behind their dusty windows, and others, weary-faced dolls, fiddles and banjos, unticking clocks, and oriental lampshades. Rusty pickup trucks were parked on the edges of the street, and telephone lines crisscrossed overhead.

Few people were out and about, but those who were walked with their heads down and their sunhats fixed over their eyes. As we ventured out of the thick of the village, farmhouses with boarded windows and loose nails popped up like buttercups, and soon, the woods grew thick again. It wasn't until we climbed the tallest hill at what must have been the very end of Starlight Valley that we came upon the mansion.

The mansion reminded me vaguely of something Mrs. Flanagan taught in a history lesson: the magnificent structures the Greeks built—the Parthenon, or the Pantheon, or whatever it was called. This was built of white marble, tall columns stretching three floors up, a balcony splitting the first and second floors. A stone path led through the garden to two stairwells circling a large door. Wisteria climbed the columns, and willows and cherry trees, pink with blossoms, tucked the palace in like sheets around a child. Pretty hydrangea bushes spotted the grounds, their flowers soft and hazy as a cloud of perfume, or perhaps the northern lights. The place could have been made of watercolors and dreams for all I could tell.

"Welcome home," said Aoife. "I trust you'll find it comfortable, Finn."

"This is all yours?" I gritted my teeth the minute I said it; how positively unsophisticated of me.

Aoife seemed unfazed, though. She squeezed my shoulders again, close to her chest and said fiercely, "You'll love it here." I could have sworn I saw fire in her eyes.

As we climbed the steps to the grand door, she added, "You shall have anything you wish for under this roof. Anything you desire will be yours. You will never shed another tear. Won't that be divine?"

By this point, I wasn't quite sure whether to say, "Yes," or "I'm only staying for a few weeks, though— right?" or "May I use the loo, please?" because the queasiness from the ride over still hadn't subsided. So, instead I said, "Probably," and cringed again at how rude the word sounded.

Aoife cast a thin-lipped smile down at me as she twisted the doorknob—gold and shaped like a bird—a swan, I realized.

The door swung open.

Warmth.

Lights.

Happiness. Pure as sugar, it lasted but a moment before my eyes adjusted to the brightness of the mansion's foyer.

And then feathers. And then swan heads. And then horror.

Chapter 20

THE WALLS WERE WHITE. The walls were not painted white. The walls were papered in feathers. Feathers so pure they could have been sewn of starlight. Stuffed swan heads lined the walls in rows like streetlamps, glassy eyes staring down at Aoife and me.

Tall marble pillars rose from the black-and-white-checkered marble floor and a chandelier hung from the ceiling with real candles alight. The candleholders were carved of gold in the shape of swan heads with very long necks, beaks spread open to keep the candles in place and swallow the wax.

At the end of the foyer, a swirly stairwell rose up to a second floor, railings made of the same gold as the chandelier. A grand piano stood in the corner, though I could see even from the door that a layer of dust coated the keys.

There was a certain smell about the place that I couldn't quite put my finger on—a creeping, crawling scent sticking to my skin like clay does after digging for it from the earth with your bare hands. The kind of scent that wouldn't wash off with water.

Aoife twirled around, feather coat flying. "What do you think, my love?"

What did I think? I thought nothing. I simply felt. What did I feel? I felt as if I were stumbling through a dream. First, because of the mother I hadn't known existed dancing before my very eyes; like a faery goddess, she felt only half real. The sort of mystery that exists only in dreamlands. She was a beautiful, frightening thing. And then, the house, like a castle for the dead. Rich in splendor, a pauper in comfort, it sent my spine shivering. It made me angry, it made me sad, it made me lonely, it made me exhilarated, it made me happy. I tasted lemon drops.

I shook my head, pretending I had only just realized Aoife's question. "I . . . it's . . . feathered—I mean festered— I mean festive—"

Aoife tossed back her head, and a prettier laugh there could not be heard. It echoed around the foyer like wind chimes in a cavern as Aoife's golden curls caught the light of the chandelier and slipped off her shoulder. "It catches your tongue, doesn't it?" she said. "Snatches your breath right out of your lungs." Aoife held up a hand and two black smudges fluttered down from the ceiling and landed on her forearm. "This is Bronwyn and Blagden," she explained. The two crows stared beadily into my eyes. "Our little pets."

Aoife led me to the stairwell, but as I was about to take the first step, she stopped me with a heavily jeweled hand— though she wore nothing on her wedding ring finger.

"Now," she said, stooping down to look me in the eye, "would you like to meet your sister?"

I froze. Da hadn't mentioned anything about sisters. *Sister.* The word beat warm in my chest. Any fear I had felt before melted away.

Aoife smiled coyly, her lips a deep, deep red. "Priscilla-Kathryn!" she called up the stairwell.

Such a strange name, I thought, as above us, a door slammed open. And then came footsteps, skipping down the stairs.

The girl's eyes, despite their effort, could not hide their shining blue behind her strawberry-blond hair. She wore a periwinkle sweater with rose-shaped buttons atop a daisy-print dress. She also wore spotless white tights instead of sporting scraped knees, and her feet were half the size of mine. Her eyebrows were raised and her lips pressed taut in annoyance as if her mother had just interrupted her from discovering a cure for polio. She picked at her pink nail polish and she did not smile. When she looked up, she did not frown, but gazed intently at me, pretty and afraid.

Aoife swept over to the banister and hurried the girl down. "Priscilla-Kathryn, meet your sister."

She stared at me.

I stared at her.

And then she smirked. "Not by blood." Her voice, unlike her mother's, was most certainly, irrefutably American. Vowels spread long and thin like ice cream melting on a sidewalk. "And they call me Posy-Kate."

"She just had a birthday—turned eleven two weeks ago," said Aoife.

"No," said Posy-Kate, "I turned eleven in February—"

Aoife's eyes glowed angrily, but she plastered on a

smile. Once more, she turned to Posy-Kate. "Well, August is when we celebrate it."

This made little sense to me, but I decided it safest to let the question slip. Instead, I said, "You're—"

"Adopted, yes," said Posy-Kate.

"Oh." I blushed. "I was going to say 'pretty.'"

"That reminds me," said Aoife to me, "*you* recently had a birthday, did you not?"

I nodded vaguely. My birthday felt so far away, though I knew it had been only a couple days before.

Aoife pulled something from inside her feather cloak—a box, tiny and wrapped in gold paper. Posy-Kate's eyes fixated on the box, mouth pressed into a dour frown. Aoife handed the box to me. I peeled off the box's tape, ripped off the gold paper, and lifted the lid.

Inside, a necklace sat atop a cloud of cotton. I picked it up, laid it flat in my palm, and let the soft metal snake through my fingers.

"It's a swan feather—real—encased in silver. You'll find I'm rather fascinated by swans."

I wanted to ask Aoife why—why was she so fascinated by swans? Did she know the story of the Children of Lir? Had Nuala told the story to her? Was Aoife the reason Nuala told the story to me? But I didn't want to press my luck, either. I didn't want to say the wrong thing. I didn't want to annoy my mother. I'd just *gotten* her, after all. No, I wouldn't lose her too. Not like Nuala, not like Darcy, not even like Da.

I laid the necklace back in its box and said, "It's lovely, thank you."

Aoife smiled. "I do hope you enjoy it."

Posy-Kate brushed in front of Aoife and demanded, "Well, are you gonna tell me your name or not?"

"Manners," snapped Aoife.

I inched back from Posy-Kate. "Finn." My voice wavered.

"'Fin'?" piped Posy-Kate, crossing her arms over her chest. "Like a fish's?"

"No," I said, and then I coughed and added, "No, I mean . . . yes. Similar to a fish fin. Like a merrow's." A merrow was a magical, mistral faery that lived beneath the sea, half human, half fish. I wasn't really like a merrow, but I thought I might like to be, at least more than I wanted to be a fish.

Posy-Kate, though, thought otherwise. She flicked at the yellowed lace on my collar, a few breadcrumbs falling to the marble floor. She tut-tutted and scoffed, "If you ask me, I think you're a fish out of water—"

"*Priscilla-Kathryn*—" shot Aoife, but to my own surprise, I cut her off.

"Perhaps a swan, then?" I said.

Three sets of lungs stood still.

Posy-Kate slowly stuck out a hand for me to shake and said silkily, "Why yes. It's a pleasure—Finbird." She smiled slyly on the word.

I did not take her hand. "Excuse me?" I breathed.

"Finbird," she repeated, withdrawing her arm. "That's what I'll call you. It'll be our little nickname. Suits you, don't it?"

There were a thousand things I could have told Posy-Kate—that Finn was already a nickname and that nicknames don't get nicknames and that even if nicknames did get nicknames, you don't make a nickname's nickname something that's twice as long as the original nickname. It was just common sense. Plus the fact that, *what kind of sorry excuse for a name is Finbird?* But the response I chose was, "Oh . . ."

Aoife quickly glided between Posy-Kate and me. "That's . . . not very interesting, Priscilla-Kathryn. Why

don't you show Finn to her room? You can help her un-
pack up there."

"You mean the guest room?" said Posy-Kate.

Aoife flushed red.

"Because she's a guest, isn't she, Mother? Just a guest.
You see, fish birds don't stay in one place for long. One
minute, they need the sea, the next, they need the air—
such . . . *nomadic* creatures. Can never make up their little
minds about what they want."

My brain fogged over as Aoife looked from me to
Posy-Kate and back to me. I wanted Posy-Kate to like
me. But what was worse was that I had *expected* her to
like me. Now I felt sunken, an old balloon tumbling
down the burning streets of Belfast. *Lonely, lonely, lonely.*

"It's fine," I said. "I'll find it on my own."

And as I climbed the spiral staircase, I realized the
smell. Blood. Stale, bitter, death-claimed blood.

Chapter 21

I FLED THE MANOR ten minutes ago. As soon as I'd dropped my suitcase on the lumpy, probably swan-feather-stuffed mattress of Aoife's guest room, I ran.

Strange things happened as I wandered down the dusty roads of Starlight Valley. Door hinges creaked. Skittish eyes peered out from curtain cracks. Chickens and goats slunk out from behind their farmhouses. Men in jeans and women in flowered skirts tiptoed out of their homes, as if a grizzly bear were sleeping nearby. It wasn't until I reached the woods that the village was in full swing, children chattering, mothers bustling, merchants flipping CLOSED signs to OPEN.

Distant fragments clattered in my ears:

"*Getch yer omelets, getch yer beer, getch yer omelets, getch yer beer.*"

"*You wouldn't* believe *the hat Margie wore to church yesterday.*"

"*Five dollars for a loaf? You thief! Two days ago they were four fifty.*"

A few whispered of an expecting mother who was sick, and others whispered ghost stories of a witch they called the "Pegwitch," but besides that, most were silent.

When I came to the edge of the forest of white-wooded aspens and deep emerald evergreens and sycamores just starting to turn golden for the fall, I opened my locket and pinched tight the single-petaled hawthorn flower. I brought it to my mouth, closed my eyes tight, and breathed these words:

"*Don't let me be lonely. Don't let me be lonely. Don't let me be lonely.*"

My breath billowed the petal. The words felt like hurricane kisses on my lips, sad and angry and rumbling louder than thunderclouds. But when I opened my eyes, the valley was silent. The hustle-bustle had faded into the distance, and not even a breeze or a bumblebee grazed the trees. I glanced down to my locket and whispered to

Margaret, Ed, and Oliver, "Fat chance," then placed the petal back inside. But as I closed the locket, the most wondrous thing happened, and that was laughter.

Just laughter. But it danced like the first snow of winter or cherry blossoms on a mid-May wind. Or will-o'-the-wisps. That was it. The laugh danced like will-o'-the-wisps, blue-flame faeries over mist-laden bogs.

I spun thrice around, cool soil plinking down my socks, but no one was there. Perhaps I had imagined it. Perhaps I had gone mad. Perhaps someone was watching me. I should have felt scared, or at the least cautious, but no. There was not a drop of malice in that laugh, and it reverberated in my heart, and my heart—my heart was warm . . .

No. The *locket* was warm.

My breath quickened. I slipped behind an aspen with a carved heart encircling the letters *J* and *B* on its bark and clicked open the locket. Behind the hawthorn flower, Ed's face was laugh struck, dimples deep set, and lanky arms slung over Oliver's and Margaret's shoulders. His teeth were crooked, half of them still baby teeth.

Something Darcy said to me rang in my ears:

"Mary says I'm wasting me time out here," Darcy had said. *"She says they en't real, the faery."*

"Neither are stories," I had told her, repeating Nuala's words. *"But that doesn't mean they don't exist."*

Curious, I thought, and closed the locket.

I continued on through the forest, leaving the weights of my new village and my new house and my new mother and my new sister at the edge of the woods. As I walked, however, I noticed something about the trees. They were named—just like my willow friends back in Donegal. Or, at least, they bore names on their bark. Most simply had carvings that said *Joe* or *Daisy* or *Greg*, but others held caterpillar-sized messages.

We've moved, Millie. Straight ahead and second house on the left, read one aspen tree, the message spinning 'round the entire circumference of the slender trunk.

Our darling Henry, we love you —Mom and Dad, read another.

The woods' lonelies ran deep through roots, pulsing in the soles of my shoes. They tangled in the treetops, dusted my shoulders as I stooped beneath the low-hanging leaves. It seemed everyone in town had a tree message for someone. Everyone had lost someone. Everyone had a hole in their heart, and every message was a story. I could have listened. I could have unfolded each story like a paper fortune-teller, unwrapped their mysteries and spun gold from their melancholies.

I could have told stories.

I could have told stories—true or make-believe, it mattered not—I could have told *stories*. The sycamores and the evergreens, my audience; the aspens, my muse. But I didn't. I read the tree messages for what they were and not a word more. Stories and I . . . well, we currently were not on pleasant terms.

Door's unlocked, read one message. *Door's always unlocked —Jeff, Connie, and Rufus.*

Where'd you go, Marlin?

I'll be better —Taylor

Dog died. Got you a llama. Come meet her? —Arnold

I'll be waiting, always —Stella

Forgive me, Ed —Nuala

I stopped short. *Nuala.* My vision filled with fog as if the greyman had found me yet again. I brushed my arms free of invisible spiders and reread the words on the aspen bark.

Nuala. I traced the words with my forefinger. It was Nuala's handwriting, letters curving the same shape as her wrinkles. Albeit, a wobbly, wriggly version of it, but it was *hers*. Tears stung my eyes and I clenched my throat to stop them from falling. I knew I was alone—but something about the messages made me feel as though a thousand ghosts were watching me with bated breath.

Questions whizzed about in my head. What had Nuala done to Ed? Why was she sorry? Had Ed forgiven her, and had they kept in touch? Or did their friendship end bullet-quick, just as Nuala's life had? And if their friendship split, had Margaret and Oliver drifted away from one or the other, or stayed close with both? What had become of them, these happy children in my locket? I bit my tongue. I should have asked her; why hadn't I *asked* her? I'd never cared much about her life, never bothered to ask about her childhood or her voyage to America. Had she gone on a boat? Did they even have planes when she was a girl? I never asked where she'd learned her stories from or what her favorite subject in school was or what was the tallest mountain she ever climbed or how Grandpa Oliver proposed. I was selfish.

The sick feeling I had felt in the taxi settled into my

stomach again. I blew a kiss to Nuala's message, turned from the tree. I half considered tying my hair ribbon to a branch so I would be able to find the tree again, but no. I wouldn't come back. The place made my skin prickle. I could have sworn I heard my bones rattle.

Yet still, there must have been tree spirits there, because my head pounded with the words: *You belong here too. You are just like us. Just like us, just like us, just like us . . .*

I needed a knife—or a pen—either would do. I patted the waist of my dress as if expecting to find pockets there—not that I ever carried around knives or pens *anyway* when I wore jeans. I bent to my knees and flicked aside pebbles and crinkly leaves and dead spiders until, at last, a needle-sharp quartz stone stabbed my thumb. I shook my wrist and scrunched my eyebrows with the pain, then plucked the stone from the ground.

When I stood, as if by magic, a blank aspen tree appeared before my eyes. Goose bumps rose on my arms as I circled the tree, footsteps soft, as if snow cushioned my feet. The tree was smaller than the others, and when I laid a hand on the pale gray bark, I found it was smooth and taut as a child's skin. I was nearly positive it had not been there before.

I took a breath and raised my hand to the bark, hand shaking. And in barely-there letters, quartz in hand, I scribbled:

Darcy

And then came the howl.

Chapter 22

WOLVES.

I had hardly scratched the "y" of Darcy's name into the aspen when the low howl sounded.

I ran. Blood thundered in my ears.

How had I even gotten in here? Everywhere I turned, a crop of identical trees popped up, and the forest seemed only to thicken the farther I ran. Sweat sunk into my Sunday dress, dripped down my legs. My vision swirled and gibberish chanted—wait . . . It *wasn't* gibberish. Was it? Through the pounding in my head, the words *find her, find her, find her* reverberated endlessly.

A gnarled sycamore root caught grasp of my shoelace, and I collapsed to my knees, the carpet of evergreen needles cushioning my fall. The world looked like a view from a merry-go-round. The sycamores melted and the aspens waltzed. The evergreens turned into baobabs, roots reaching for the sky instead of the ground. I squeezed shut my eyes to stop the dizziness, but still the words pounded relentlessly: *Find her, find her, find her.*

"FIND WHO?" I cried aloud, but I already knew.

AH-WHOOOO!

The howling was close, and I curled into a ball, twigs and thorns jabbing my arms, and I crossed my arms over my face—but wait. It wasn't a wolf. It was a whistle. It was—

WHOOSH!

Something thin and sharp whizzed past my cheek, the rush of cool air stinging my sweat-drenched forehead. I froze, held my breath.

I peeked open one eye. The swirling had stopped, but old greyman's mist had thickened, and with it came . . . train tracks. Smooth silver tracks running far as I could see, and in the distance, a scarlet train rumbled, smoke billowing out the engine's top. The whistle blared a low howl that didn't sound quite so wolflike now that I could see the train for what it was. But where was it coming from? I didn't remember seeing a train station anywhere in town, and the valley was surrounded by those odd thorn trees—the ones that had sealed up after I entered. Even the taxi driver had said there was no way in.

Something was falling. Through the gold-spattered treetops it tumbled, bouncing over branches and screeching a song akin to that of a banshee mourning at her wash pail. I squinted as the thing plummeted toward the tracks, and then went still, lying limp on the silver tracks. It was a white thing, a trembling thing, with a stick of sorts protruding from its middle.

My vision flicked from the train to the creature. *Move!* I wanted to shout, but there was something about the creature's shaking that told me it couldn't. I had to save it. The train blared closer as finally my feet caught up with my mind, and I snapped upright. My legs felt like jellyfish, but I stumbled over the roots and branches, closer to the silver tracks. Mist thickened with every step I took, but the train's fog light shone through like a beacon, and I followed it until I met the tracks.

There. The white creature was only a few paces off. I stumbled along the tracks as the chugging of the train grew louder. Perhaps the creature reflected the train's fog light, for it seemed to glow brighter the nearer I drew. At last, the creature came into full view.

It was a swan. I knelt down, glancing toward the train as its whistle blasted again. The swan's feathers stood on end and its stomach jolted with unsteady breaths. And there, stuck in its left wing, was an arrow. Blood stained the feathers around the wound and dripped onto the silver track. The swan's beak was nibbling furiously at something on the track—a piece of wire on the track tangled around its foot.

"It's all right," I cooed, but my voice wavered unconvincingly. "I—I'm gettin' you out of here."

I wrapped my arms around the swan's cold belly and it screeched with agony, but did not snap at me. I recoiled, heart pounding, and glanced toward the train again. It was hardly a hundred meters away.

Someone shouted—a boy—ordering me to please get my freakish backside off of the tracks. Except he didn't say *please*, and he didn't say *freakish*, and he most certainly did not say *backside*.

I hunched toward the wire wrapped around the swan's ankle and dug my nails underneath it as the swan howled again. The wire clung tight as a cross-stitch, digging into the swan's leathery skin.

"It's a *bird*, and it's good as dead anyway. Just let it be, you stupid girl!" cried the boy again.

My fingers began to tremble in rhythm to the vibrating tracks. I glanced behind myself and froze; the train was hardly a tree's length away, but the faster I thought the words *slow down, slow down, slow down*, the faster the train seemed to approach. We were done for. Both of us.

And then came the icy *whoosh*, just like before, as something whizzed past my cheek and into—

The swan. A second arrow plunged into her foot, blood spattering onto my dress. I tugged at the arrow and it released, pulling with it a wad of tangled wire. I tossed it to the side as the voice shouted again. "Come *on!*" it said.

I looked up, and a boy's face—sallow and sunken— appeared through my blurred and swirling vision. It scowled down at me. He stretched out a sweaty hand and I grabbed it with my right, dragging the swan with my left.

He yanked, and we all tumbled into the pine needle carpet as the train rattled by. I held the swan close to my chest, the first arrow in its wing jabbing into my shoulder. My breath leapt like skipping stones. When the train disappeared into the fog and all became quiet in the forest again, I leaned into the swan's breast to listen for its heartbeat. It was a murmur of a thing, trilling hummingbird quick and fading fast.

"She's hurt bad," I muttered, now tugging at the bloody arrow. At last I yanked it out of the swan's wing, blood oozing through the feathers, turning the wing bright crimson. The swan's muscles tensed, eyes drooped—and then its neck went limp, falling back onto my chest, unconscious.

I twirled around to the boy, saying, "We've got to find h—"

I froze. A hunter—spider-limbed and pinch-faced—was crouched behind me, bow slung over his shoulder and arrows scattered on the pine needles.

"You did this."

Chapter 23

"MIND YOU, I SAVED YOUR LIFE—*and* its." Sojourn gestured to the swan.

"You?" I scoffed. "You weren't the one nose to nose with a massive train hurtling your way. This never would have even happened if you hadn't shot her out of the sky. What's she ever done to you?"

Sojourn shrugged. "Got to kill to eat."

My stomach squirmed at the thought of eating a creature as majestic as a swan.

Sojourn must have caught my expression of disgust, because he added, "I don't eat them. I sell 'em. The mayor up on the hill collects 'em like postage stamps. Batty old woman, if you ask me, but she pays well. Been working for her for years. . . . I believe you've made acquaintances?"

My cheeks burned. "How d'you know that? And—and Aoife's the mayor?"

But Sojourn did not answer. "'Sides," he continued, "if it hadn't been for you, the swan would've died a quick death. Now it'll suffer. It's only a matter of time 'fore she snuffs it, you know."

"No she won't. I'll save her. I'll find help—a vet—or—or I'll nurse her back to health myself if I've got to. And stop calling her 'it'!"

"How're you so sure it's a girl anyway?"

"I've studied swans for years, bogbrain." It wasn't like me to drop insults, but Sojourn, that Sojourn brought out the worst in me. "Females are smaller and have thinner necks, and the knob on her bill is smaller too." I huffed and propped up the swan's head over my shoulder. Then I heaved myself to my feet, knees quivering with the extra weight of the swan. "C'mon," I said. "I don't know the town, so you'll have to show me the way."

But Sojourn did not get to his feet. He stayed put longer than I cared for, stuttering, "Finn—you—just wait—"

"What?" I snapped. "We've got to go. Come on."

"But Finn, you don't understand—"

I shook a piece of hair out of my face and fired, "I understand perfectly. If you don't want to help me, fine. But I'm getting this swan help whether you like it or not. She's not going to end up another one of Aoife's wall hangings." And I took off through the forest, aspens blurring past. And though I hadn't a clue which way to go, I figured the forest couldn't last forever, and the valley wasn't terribly big. I'd reach the village somehow. I turned back but once to see Sojourn snatch up his arrows and flail after me, hollering, "Wait!"

But I did not wait. I ran and ran, and as I did, I whispered in the swan's ear, "I've got you, girl." And then, softer—so not Sojourn, nor the trees, not the ghosts, nor even I could hear—I breathed, "I've got you, Child of Lir. I've got you, Ena."

AFTER WHAT FELT LIKE HOURS, the trees began to thin, and I stumbled out to a cliff overlooking a ravine. A red-berried tree grew there, hunched over the edge, and I collapsed against it, cradling the swan in my tired arms.

My fingers had become numb with their grip on the swan, and my vision swirled and doubled. I closed my eyes to stop the dizziness and leaned my ear against the swan's chest again. Her heart still beat, but faintly.

From within the forest, a distant shout sounded. "Stop! *Stop!* You haven't a clue what you're doing!"

Then out tumbled Sojourn, gangly legs swiveling and long arms drooping. He fell to his knees on a patch of thistle, only to yelp with the pain of the spiky plant. His black-widow eyes watered as he sprang away from the thistle and clambered onto a small boulder opposite me, reaching dramatically for the top of the stone like a near-drowning victim would a lifeboat.

He wheezed out the words, "Aoife . . . will kill . . . the swan . . . the minute . . . she sets eyes on it—"

"*Her*—"

Sojourn attempted to roll his eyes, but they simply lolled to the side with exhaustion. Once he caught his breath, he said more coherently, "Give *her* to me. There en't a vet for a hundred miles of the place, no less within the valley—not that you'd be able to leave if you wanted to. No one leaves the valley without Aoife's word. I'll take care of the swan."

I eyed Sojourn suspiciously. "She needs practiced hands. She needs love and warmth and lots of care. No offense, but you're not exactly the motherly sort, now, are you?" I nodded to his satchel of arrows sagging at his waist.

And then Sojourn did something most unexpected. He did something kind. He did something brave.

He slung off his bow and satchel and handed them to me. "I promise," he said. "I promise I'll take care of her."

Sojourn's eyes lost their smirk, and for the first time, they filled with . . . honesty. Despite the pounding, the pleading, *I'm trusting you, I'm trusting you, I'm trusting you*, inside my head, no words landed on my tongue. So, I simply took the bow and arrows, and eased the swan over to Sojourn's lap.

He tore a piece off his already-tattered sleeve and wrapped it 'round the swan's wing to stop the bleeding and create a sling. "See?" he said. "She's looking better already." He struggled to stand up with the new weight, and when he did, he nearly toppled over backward and his knees bowed precariously. All the same, he nodded and said, "Go on now. Aoife'll want to know where you've been. But one piece of advice, love . . . don't tell her."

It wasn't until I was halfway into the village that I realized what tree I had been leaning against. I pinched open my locket and shielded the photograph from the sun's glare with my hand. The hawthorn tree Margaret, Ed, and Oliver sat atop curved over a ravine, branches bowed but strong. It was a perfect match.

Chapter 24

I REEKED OF BLOOD AND SWEAT, even worse than the already acrid smell of Aoife's feathered walls. High-heeled footsteps clattered down the marble staircase. Aoife's feather coat swished into view, followed by a fluff of disheveled golden hair. When she caught sight of me, she swept down the stairs in one movement and embraced me. Long fingernails trailed through my hair as I breathed in her sugar-plum perfume.

But as Aoife released me, her jaw hardened.

"Foolish girl!" she flared. "You're just as wild as that so-called mother of yours—" She stopped short, sucking in her scarlet mouth as if she'd just swallowed a lemon whole.

"I—I just went for a stroll in the woods, I didn't mean no harm."

"Well, you did do harm," shot Aoife. She then took a large breath. When her shoulders fell an inch and she regained her composure, she said through gritted teeth, "You must never leave the manor."

I stepped back, light-headedness washing over me. "Never leave?"

Aoife threw up her hands and began to march back up the stairs. "Not now, not ever, *never*. Not without my supervision anyway."

"What about—school? And food? And—and plain fresh air?"

"You will be educated by the finest tutors, cared for by the finest nannies. For heaven's sake, your bedroom is lined with gold-rimmed windows. Now, what is on your dress? And what is that *smell*?" Aoife began to pace across the marble floor. "You need a bath—no, you need a *consequence*." Her cheeks reddened as her anger rose, voice reverberating off the high ceiling. "No pudding tonight—no—no *supper* tonight. Off to bed straightaway, and not even a thought of nicking something from the kitchens; the cooks will all . . ."

Aoife's eyes fell to my neck, and her voice trailed away. Once again, her temper softened. "My," she murmured, shaking her movie star curls as if her anger were made of dandruff. She floated down the few steps she had climbed. "I—I don't know what's gotten into me . . . Of course you shall eat supper with us. All is forgiven, my darling." She slunk closer, a strange hunger chained behind her eyes. She bent to my eye level. Her neck twitched as she swallowed and said, "Why aren't you wearing your necklace, darling?"

I narrowed my eyes. "What necklace?"

"Why, your birthday gift. The swan feather one I gave you, of course."

"Oh—oh, I left it in my bedroom."

"Never mind, I've got it here," and Aoife pulled from her coat pocket the welcome gift.

My lips felt like they were sucking an icicle. "You went through my things?" I managed.

Aoife ignored me. "Allow me," she said.

And Aoife reached behind my neck and unclasped the silver locket. She withdrew it and the chain dribbled into her palm. I reached for it, but quick as a vulture on prey, Aoife snapped the locket in two. The hawthorn petal fluttered to the floor, and I snatched it up, and then lunged for the locket, shouting, "No! Please, that's Nuala's!"

But Aoife swished away like a master dancer. She pocketed the pieces of the locket and said, "No need to fuss, darling. You don't want that old thing weighing down your pretty face. People will think you're destitute."

Oh yes, I wanted to say, *all the people I'm not allowed to see because I must remain within the manor.*

She leaned forward, a smile plastered on her face, and hooked the silver-cased swan feather necklace around my neck. "Much better," she said. There was something about her teeth that reminded me of a boggart's—sharp and sweet-turned-wicked, for boggarts were spritely faeries that would turn sinister at the slightest vexation. Milk served without honey or needle and thread moved to a new closet, and you would wake up to a face of boils.

"Now, be a good girl and go change into something fresh. I'm sure Priscilla-Kathryn will have something that fits."

I stared at Aoife, hard and cold. Her smile did not falter, and she chirped, "Don't be glum, darling. I'll have Nancy cook us a special dinner—potatoes and sausage perhaps, and banoffee pie for pudding. Something that feels like home." She kissed the top of my head and added, "I love you."

I swallowed back my tears. "I love you too," I said, voice stony. I averted my eyes from hers as I swept past and hurried up the stairs.

So it was. Each dawn, I woke to the cawing of Aoife's two pet crows, Bronwyn and Blagden, and ate breakfast in the drawing room with Aoife and Posy-Kate. At nine o'clock, Mrs. Carleton arrived with her books and chalkboard and taught arithmetic and English, and at noon, Miss Fletcher came and taught history and French. For late-afternoon lessons, Mr. Randal brought a violin and tried ever so hard to "scrub the fiddle out of me" with minuets and gavottes, concertos and sonatas.

At sunset, Chef Nancy would call us all for supper, and I would eat in silence as Posy-Kate chastised my outfits or my hair or my manners. And every night, Aoife kissed me good night and said she loved me more than the stars, more than the moon, more than her thumbs, and more than the hair on her head. Then she would tuck me in and double-lock the door. To be loved, I decided, is a dangerous thing indeed.

All the while, even Aoife took habit of calling me Finbird. The maids began to catch on, and it wasn't long before the few pieces of mail I received (mainly adverts preceded with the words "To the parent of") addressed me as "Miss Finbird O'Dálaigh."

One week spun into two, and two spun into three, and through it all, I heard not a peep from Da.

I grew tired. I grew lonely.

I thought of the swan. I thought of Darcy, if she'd been found yet. I thought of Nuala and I thought of the hawthorn. I thought of Sojourn. I thought of Da, who still hadn't written to me. I missed his handwriting. The scar above his lip and his kisses on my forehead. I missed the sunshine, the warmth on my shoulders seeping into my bones. I missed the rain and I missed the trees and the sound of village chatter. I missed the sound of laughter.

Some nights, I would open up all seven of my windows just to feel the wind on my skin. And when the first frost came in mid-September, I stayed up all night and breathed in the air. The crisp, cool air that reminded me so much of blackberry pies and long walks in the willow glades and peat burning in the hearth and sneaky sips of Nuala's hot Irish coffee. My fingers would go numb and my teeth would chatter and my toes would quiver, but I would not give in to blankets or bathrobes. I would let the cold sink in. Let it sail me away, carry me until, at last, I scraped the shores of dreamland. And always, I dreamed of Ireland. Always, I dreamed of the little house at the edge of the willows in Donegal, where nothing ever happened, yet adventures roamed free for those who called it home.

But what frightened me most was this: I got used to the smell of blood.

Chapter 25

ONE NIGHT, I STAYED UP until the stars dulled and the moon sank low and the sky corners collected dust the color of plum blossoms. I played a Peter, Paul and Mary record that was left in the record player in the guest room, and I wept and I prayed, but most of all I forgot. I forgot my disdain for stories, the danger and the loss and the loneliness they brought. I forgot and I wrote. I wrote down stories, the stories Nuala would tell me before bed and at cliff edges or wildflower meadows, the stories she had handed down to me, and each one I addressed to Da. The last story, I scribbled at the top of the page with shaking fingers:

The Children of Lir

I told of the children-turned-swans just the way I told it to Darcy, but this time, when I told of the eldest child, Ena, I imagined the swan from the train. I imagined her eyes, dark and afraid. And as I wrote, the song "500 Miles" chimed through the record player. The song lilted:

If you miss the train I'm on, you will know that I am gone . . .

I told of Lir mourning the loss of his wife, Aobh, as the twins, Fiachra and Conn, were born.

You can hear the whistle blow a hundred miles . . .

I told of the wedding bells. Of Aoife marrying Lir, of Aoife holding a child of her own. A child named Finnuala.

A hundred miles, a hundred miles, a hundred miles, a hundred miles . . .

I told of how Ena took Finnuala from Aoife's loving arms, how Lir left his wife without home or family out of false love.

Lord, I'm one, Lord, I'm two, Lord, I'm three, Lord, I'm four, Lord, I'm five hundred miles from my home . . .

I told of Aoife taking the children to their half-faery grandmother. To Inis Eala, to the hawthorn tree, where the elder children ate the berries to save Finnuala.

Not a shirt on my back, not a penny to my name . . .

I told of the half-faery grandmother. I told of her cradling the life-fading children. Saving them with berries of the same hawthorn, these ones blessed instead of cursed.

Lord, I can't go a-home this a-way . . .

I told of the berries turning the pale-limbed children into swans. I told of how they flew away.

If you miss the train I'm on, you will know that I am gone . . .

I told of the half faery sending her daughter across the globe. Banishing her from her home.

You can hear the whistle blow a hundred miles.

I left out the part about Aoife causing Aobh's death—how Aoife grew a thornbush in her sister's heart with her faery magic of life. Because despite all the people Aoife had hurt, I knew she would want to go home.

And I swear, through the feathered walls I could hear my mother weeping for all the years she had lost with me, and for her infertility that followed her loss of me. I could have *sworn* I heard it. And it hurt, because despite it all, I understood. So I turned the record louder. And despite all the people I hurt, I wanted to go home. Those were the final words I wrote, and I wrote them over and over and over.

I want to go home.
I want to go home.
I want to go home.

❧

WHEN THE CROWS CAWED, I trundled weary-eyed down to the drawing room for breakfast and sat down at the table. Pushing my food in circles around my plate, I realized how foolish I had been. I wouldn't be able to send the stories. I wasn't allowed to go to the post office, no less out the back door. At least . . . not alone.

"Ma?" I said, looking up at Aoife. I had discovered that the more I called Aoife *Ma* rather than *Miss* or *Madam* or *Ma'am*, the more likely I was to get out of violin lessons or stay up an extra half hour.

"The Finbird *talks*," ogled Posy-Kate.

She shoveled a forkful of scrambled eggs into her mouth, then leaned in close as if she were telling a ghost story and repeated, "The Finbird . . . *it talks.*"

"Hush, Priscilla-Kathryn," snapped Aoife. She turned her attention to me and smiled. "Yes, what is it, darling?"

"I wondered if I might stop by the post office. I've

some letters I thought I might send to folk back home."

Posy-Kate choked on her orange juice. Aoife contorted her smile so it stretched twice as wide as a normal person's.

Posy-Kate scoffed. "Who'd want to hear from *you*? I know *I'd* rather receive mail from a dirty bird than—oh wait—that's right, you *are* a bird. A grimy, covered-in-pond-scum waterfowl. Isn't that right, *Finbird*?" she cackled, tossing a piece of sausage to the crows at the feet of the table. They pounced on the meat like vultures, savagely tearing at the carpet with their beaks. The moment one believed it had won the prize, the other would peck it out of its greedy little mouth.

"Enough, girls," shot Aoife. "And don't feed the crows; they're already fat as it is, the wee beasts." Immediately, Aoife reddened, as she so often did, at the slip of her colloquial Irish. She turned to me and added, "If you have mail, simply give it to Nancy. I'm sure she'd send whatever you wish."

"I'd like to see the letters off myself, if it's all the same to you."

Aoife took a sip of her tea, then said, "It isn't." She dabbed her mouth and turned to Posy-Kate. "Priscilla-Kathryn, did you finish your—Dorothy! Leave that plate be. Good Lord, it's hard to find decent help these days."

"Sorry, ma'am," squeaked the maid, scurrying back into the kitchen.

Aoife returned her gaze to Posy-Kate, but I piped in. "Has there . . . By any chance . . . There hasn't been any word from my da?"

Aoife's jaw twitched, and she tipped up her chin. "Not a word. Priscilla-Kathryn, use your napkin, please."

"Sorry, Mom."

"Now, Priscilla-Kathryn—"

"I just thought he'd have written by now. He promised he would, and he never breaks his word. Besides that, I was supposed to be back in Ireland by now."

Aoife's neck tensed as if she were holding her breath, lips parted, before she finally said delicately, "Has it occurred to you that perhaps your father no longer wishes you around?"

Posy-Kate snickered. My fingertips went cold and I dropped my spoon into my porridge. "What's that supposed to mean?" I said.

"Oh, darling . . ." cooed Aoife, bending close to embrace me, but I pulled away. I shoved back my chair, tossed my silk napkin onto the table, and dashed for the stairs.

Don't be stupid, I thought, *of course he loves you*. But the trouble was, there wasn't a soul left to affirm this, nor was there a speck of evidence to support it. As much as I *hoped* Aoife was wrong, that Da still loved me, still longed for me, there was a possibility—perhaps even a probability— that yes, Aoife, yes, she was right.

Don't be stupid, don't be stupid, don't be stupid, I thought as I raced up the stairs, trying to bottle the thoughts inside my stomach. But there was just something about Aoife's voice, the slickness of it, that weaseled its way into my brain like a bookworm, chewing at all that I knew to be true.

When I came to my bedroom door, I stopped but for a moment. I wanted to be alone. Despite the loneliness burning in my chest, all I wanted was to be *alone*. Truly alone, where no one would find me. I raced past the door and down the feather-walled corridor, up winding stair-well after stairwell until I found myself thoroughly lost.

The room I came upon was set off from the rest of the house—a sort of attic perhaps, or an old servants' quarter. It was bare, except for a single black curtain draped along an oddly lightless window. It was perhaps the only un-feathered room in the manor, walls simple white with water stains by the window and mothballs in the corners. A chill rattled my bones, slunk into the small of my back like snow slipping down my blouse. I walked on a sea of cobweb castles, dust billowing like pixie dust beneath my feet.

"*Hello*," I whispered.

My breath turned to smoke in the air, and my voice echoed back:

Hello, hello, hello . . .

"*Hello?*"

I froze. That surely was not an echo. My throat seemed to have frosted over, but I scraped out a feeble "*Hello?*" again.

"*Helloooooo*," repeated the voice, soft and small. "Posy-Kate, is that you?"

"No," I said.

Silence.

A shiver struck my ribs, and I chattered out, "It's Finbir—Finn. It's Finn."

Silence.

And then a squeak. A flighty, fluttery sound that I knew oh so dearly. "*Finn?* Finnuala O'Dálaigh-Sé?"

"Yes," I breathed.

With a *pound*, the floorboards shuddered, and I could tell the voice's owner had leapt with joy. "I knew you'd come for me!" And then came the banging behind the black curtain, as if someone were throwing pebbles at the window.

I trod closer, each footstep sounding like a *crash, zoink, ping!* despite how high on my tiptoes I walked. *I shouldn't be here*, my mind repeated, but my fingers took no mind and tugged at the curtain. It felt like river water beneath my fingertips. I closed my eyes and pretended I was dipping my hand into the River Boyne, as I so often did back in Ireland. I could smell the freshness mingling with the farm animal dung, hear the cows lowing in the green, green fields and the oaks rustling in the wind. Cool breeze in my hair, a lemon drop on my tongue. If you're away long enough, anything can make you miss home.

I pulled back the curtain and opened my eyes. The window, well, the window was not a window at all.

Chapter 26

IF YOU DO NOT KNOW ABOUT TREES, you likely would not know that yew trees grow in graveyards. They grow tall and wide and house robins in the springtime. Well, the door behind the curtain in the hidden room above the manor was made from the wood of a yew tree. I could tell by the smell of it—the smell of death and sorrows. It was rough, unfinished wood, and when I touched it, I had to pluck a splinter from my palm with my fingernails.

"Won't you come in, Finn?" bubbled the familiar voice again. It sounded like it was coming from just behind the doorknob. "Oh, please do. Please come in."

I twisted the knob, and out tumbled a tiny girl with hair the color of raven's feathers and eyes like storm clouds over Connemara. My heart jigged double time, and tears spurted from my eyes. I melted to my knees and embraced Darcy Brannon with all my might.

When she squeaked with breathlessness, I withdrew and blubbered, "I—I thought I'd never see you again. I—I thought you were . . . oh, it doesn't matter!" I sighed and choked out, "I'm so sorry, Darcy. I'm *so sorry.*"

"Why're you sorry, Finn? You en't got nothin' to be sorry for."

And then logic dawned on me, and I tilted my head up at Darcy and asked, "What are you doing here? Why're you—who brought you here? Who put you here?"

"*Shh,*" hushed Darcy. "C'mon in, I'll explain everythin'. But we mustn't be heard by *her.*"

I nodded, thoroughly confused, and followed Darcy into the cavernous room behind the yew door. I coughed out a cloud of dust as I crossed the threshold, yet a distinct pine aroma pleased my nose. The room must have been a sort of attic-turned-conservatory. The walls were made of slanting, sloping wood, and beams crisscrossed the ceiling like telephone wires, but strung across them were—I gasped in horror—barbed wire? No.

They were vines. Thorn-speckled vines and thick-wooded tree branches zigzagged the ceiling and the walls, collecting in piles in the corners like rope. They appeared to be exactly the same mystifying species as the thorn trees that encircled Starlight Valley.

"What are they for?" I breathed, my voice echoing 'round the room.

Darcy glanced up to the ceiling where I was staring, and shrugged. "Oh. Dunno, really. Aoife grows them, I s'pose."

I gazed around the rest of the room, a sick feeling squeezing my insides ever tighter. A lumpy, dull gray cot was perched in the corner beside a flickering candle, and a few shafts of light filtered in from cracks in the ceiling (under which pails were set to collect rainwater). A minuscule bathroom was tucked in the corner, and piles of old toys, books, and records cluttered the walls. The most cheerful thing about the place was a wide fireplace set with three glass swan figurines on the mantelshelf. But that too was falling apart, crumbling bricks collecting in the hearth. In the dim light, I could see Darcy's porcelain dollface was marred with ash and silt, and her hair was matted. Her eyes, still shining, sunk back in her head.

"Leave the door ajar, or we'll be stuck here till Posy-Kate comes with lunch," said Darcy.

My footsteps creaked as I walked. "You know Posy-Kate?" I whispered. "She's a horrid girl. Ciara Cassidy times a thousand worse."

Darcy bit her lip. "She en't that bad."

"She is *so*. They call me 'Finbird,' both of 'em, and they make fun of my clothes and my hair and the way I talk too."

Darcy turned away, and I had to lean down to hear her say, "She brings me food. She brings me water. She sews me blankets."

"She sews?" I muttered, more to myself. That would explain the quirky patterns and peculiar sweaters and buttons Posy-Kate so often wore—so different from her mother with swan-feather jackets and what I had come to realize were swan-bill high heels.

Darcy nodded and pulled me by the hand over to the cot. She then threw back the cot's gray sheet to reveal a quilt of vibrantly colored mismatched fabrics—some flowery cotton, others silk, and yet more, weathered denim—appeared beneath. My mind flashed to the quilt Nuala had made long ago. I remembered that blackened patch and wondered if perhaps it belonged to Aoife.

"Almost as well as Nuala, if I might be so bold. How is she, anyway? I can't *believe* she sent you here. I mean, I knew they were looking for you—matter o' fact, that's how I ended up here—but that's old news. Hey, what's that feather doin' 'round your neck? Doesn't suit you, Finn, not one bit."

I stifled a laugh as Darcy shuffled over to a jewelry box balanced between a stack of envelopes and a record player. She opened it up and withdrew something that glimmered in the candlelight.

"I thought my life was full-out over. But then I found *this*. I tried to mend it with some old packing tape I found," said Darcy, "but Aoife caught me—she comes up every now an' then an' checks that it's still here. And me. I told her straight out it belongs to you an' no one else, but that Aoife wouldn't listen, now would she? She's a grumpy lady. Anyway, here it is." She skipped over to me and dropped Nuala's broken locket in my unsuspecting palms. I fumbled to catch it, then held my breath. Despite the goose bumps dappling my arms, warmth trickled down my fingers and into my chest.

I brought the locket to my nose and breathed in the smell of burnt brambleberry pie and rosemary soap. It smelled like Nuala. It smelled like home. Margaret, Ed, and Oliver gazed up at me, and there was something about their smiles that appeared more joyous than ever. The hawthorn tree seemed to waltz in a wind before my eyes, though perhaps it was simply the dizziness that had descended on me, and I remembered the tree I had come to before. The one with the scarlet berries, where I had entrusted Sojourn with the injured swan. Ena. It was, I realized, the one place I had visited that felt like home. I longed to return.

"Imagine Nuala's face when she finds out what Aoife did to the locket—an' you an' me. You're stick thin, Finn, stick thin!" Darcy chirped. "That Aoife has it comin' to her, I tell you."

"Darcy . . ." I looked up at her, eyes spritely as ever. Guilt rumbled the pit of my stomach.

"Hmm?"

"Nuala . . . Nuala's dead."

Darcy's mouth dropped. "What?" She shook her head and added, "No. Don't be silly, Finn. Nuala doesn't die, and it's not nice to fib about such things."

"It's my fault. She was saving me after . . . and then we had to go to . . . I was stupid, okay? Really, really stupid."

"Oh . . ." Darcy's eyes fell, and her throat tightened as she slumped onto the cot.

I slumped down too, a low-hanging thorn vine scraping my chin on the way, and wrapped an arm around Darcy's shoulder.

She sniffed and whispered, "But I like Nuala."

"Me too." I sighed, and the lump in my throat rose again.

No. I would not cry in front of Darcy. I had to be her rock, not the other way around.

"Did you bury her?" asked Darcy.

"We—" I stopped short.

No. We hadn't buried her. Hadn't even had a proper ceremony. Father Cooley hadn't visited, and I didn't even know where Nuala's body was. Was it being kept at a hospital? A funeral home? Was she cremated yet? Had they buried her without me or scattered her in a river or sent her ashes up to the stars in a floating lantern?

"I'm sorry, Darcy," was all I could say. "I'm sorry. If I hadn't told the story . . . If I hadn't heard the story . . . If I hadn't swam to the isle . . ."

Darcy's face popped up, tearstained and blotched red. "You made it to the *isle?*"

I nodded, pulling from my sweater pocket the hawthorn flower I had rescued from the locket. "An' all I've got to show for it is a dried-up bit o' hawthorn flower an' a dead Nuala." I didn't mention the story Nuala gave me on that isle, but it occurred to me that that story—the one about Nuala immigrating to Starlight Valley and befriending the children from the locket—had been the last story she'd ever told me. I'd already given Darcy the Children of Lir story; I'd keep this one for myself awhile.

I shook away the memories. "Won't you tell me how you got here, Darcy? Won't you tell me what all has happened?"

And then Darcy, my Darcy told me a tale.

Chapter 27

"I CRIED FOR THE SWAN, and he came. I was sinking like a—like a rocket ship. You know, like if the sky and the earth were flipped so the rocket blasted down instead of up. Anyway, point is, I was drowning. There was another too. Another girl, I mean. I told the swan to fetch her too, but he must'a been hard of hearing or the thunder must'a been too loud, 'cause after he pulled me from the sea, he flew right over the girl.

"Well, I held tight to the swan's feathers and rode him like horse. He was larger than most swans, though when I looked at him in the sea, he had appeared normal sized. I told him thank you very much for saving me, my house is number four, Muggins Drive. Then I fell asleep, real deep. And when I woke, I was not in Ireland anymore.

"I was bruised, covered in pine needles and a few massive thorns, and my arms and legs were cut, and I hadn't the foggiest why. A woman was carrying me. She stroked my hair and called me her Finnuala. And then I fell asleep again.

"When I woke, the woman gave me chicken noodle soup and two scoops of chocolate ice cream, which are my two most favorite things if you didn't already know. I was lying on a fancy gold bed in a room with many windows and lots of feathers, an' there were one older kid beside me bed. The woman kept callin' me Finnuala an' told me to speak. Unfortun'ly my throat wasn't workin' properly. Well, the next day my throat *was* working properly, an' I told the lady, 'Thanks a million for the soup an' ice cream, but my name en't Finnuala. I've a friend named that, but not me, no sir-ee.' I guess she didn't like that much, because I didn't get any more soup or chocolate ice cream after that, an' she didn't talk too sweet to me neither anymore. So, that's how I ended up here. A maid cleaned up the pretty room like it'd been infested with dung beetles, an' Aoife stuffed me up here with the rubbish and the bats. That's all there really is to tell."

Darcy's eyes were wide and bright as the summer solstice sky. In Ireland, the sun stays alight until past eleven o'clock at night on the solstice. But when she turned to me, the rain clouds cornering her irises rolled in and she hung her head. "You don't believe me."

That was true. I'd seen a train appear as if from nowhere, a thorn tree open and close on its own accord, and a swan seemingly save a child from the sea, yet I could not bring myself to believe Darcy. I wanted to. I wanted, dearly, to believe, and no doubt I would have before things changed. Before everything changed. Before I stopped believing in stories.

Perhaps it had been a military submarine that had found Darcy, mistaking her for an American tourist, and sending her to Starlight Valley—*no*, I thought. That seemed even less possible than Darcy's story. Of all the millions of places in the world Darcy could have ended up, how had she managed to arrive in the exact same country, the exact same state, the exact same town, and the exact same *house* as me? Why wouldn't they have simply brought her to shore, back to Nanny Hurley? It all seemed too improbable to believe. Too serendipitous. Quite. Something was off about the whole thing, yet still . . . magic. Magic, that sly, slippery, slink of a word; it made my arm hair stand on end. *Real magic.* Ha! Not a chance.

"No," I replied at last. I could not bring myself to believe, but I would not lie to Darcy, not anymore. I slid her up onto my lap and added, "But I believe in you." *And Darcy*, I thought to myself, *I believe you will discover a way for me to see the truth.* "You know, the other girl didn't die."

"What other girl?"

"The girl in the water. The girl in the sea . . . she was me. That's who the swan was looking for—me. For some reason, he got us mixed up. He wasn't expecting two people to be going to Inis Eala that night. That's why he brought you here."

The story of the Children of Lir thumped in my chest. Could it be true? Could it be real? Could it be possible? But if Darcy really *had* flown a swan bareback to America, and if the swans really *were* the Children of Lir, and if Aoife really was the stepmother witch, and if I . . . if I really *were* the youngest Child . . . then why had the swans taken Darcy—who they believed to be me—straight to Aoife? Why would they hand their youngest sibling, who they sacrificed themselves for, over to the one person from whom they wished to protect her? And then I remembered . . . Aoife was a healer—a faery healer, the most powerful of all sorts. Darcy was good as dead when the swans found her in the sea. They took her back to have her healed by Aoife.

When I snapped to, Darcy was chattering on about how now *I* was her story keeper for *her* story, which practically made her a storyteller herself, and how once she was back in Donegal, she was going to tell Mr. McCann and her dance teacher, Miss Eileen, and Nanny Hurley her new tale, and perhaps even another story that had yet to happen. "Mrs. Flanagan'll probably say she never heard a story so ridiculous, and Mr. McCann'll probably say somethin' like, 'Oh, jolly good, Darcy Brannon, that's a mighty fine tale you tell.'"

I giggled. "He en't British, Dar—"

Footsteps. Slow, soprano-pitched footsteps echoed from the other side of the yew door. Darcy's eyes glazed over. "You can't be seen, Finn," she whispered. "Not with me."

My muscles locked, and my bones stuck together like left-out-in-the-sun lemon drops. Darcy's shoulders hunched, soot-stained cheeks whitened. *She's coming, she's coming, she's coming*, rattled my brain.

"Please," croaked Darcy.

Hide, hide, hide.

Chapter 28

MY EYES FLICKED SIDE TO SIDE, up, down, and across the thorn-draped attic. There had to be a nook, a cranny, a niche, a crevice. I first, of course, considered under the bed, but the mattress was far too close to the floor for me to slide under. Then I considered behind the door, but no, Aoife was not daft; that would be the first place she checked if she were looking for me.

"It'll be all right," I assured Darcy, but in my mind, I squealed: *We're toast!*

My breath snagged in my throat. *Toast!* My eyes darted toward the fireplace and up the blackened chimney. I pocketed the two pieces of the broken locket and scurried over to it as Darcy said, "Wha—"

"Shh."

Yes, it would do splendidly. I crouched to my knees, charcoal smearing my palms as I crawled into the hearth. The smell of smoke enveloped me, and it was all I could to do to keep from gagging. Once inside, I stood and tapped blindly around the chimney in search of loose bricks to climb. There were none, but—*ouch*. A thorn pricked my finger, and I grasped a rough, twisty piece of wood. As my eyes adjusted to the dark, I could make out a winding branch cascading down the chimney. It was scorched black and speckled with massive thorns, but— I yanked on it—sturdy. The footsteps outside grew louder, heavier.

I braced myself for the pain, then clutched the branch with all my strength and pulled myself up a half foot, swinging my legs to the wall of the hearth to anchor myself. My palms quivered with pain at each new position, thorns scraping my skin and tangling my hair. I wriggled up another half foot and continued as so, hand after hand, like I would monkey bars at a child's playground.

And like Father Christmas, I climbed up the chimney.

THE YEW DOOR SLAMMED OPEN. The chimney rattled, sending a cloud of soot down into my eyes. My arms quivered with the strength of holding on to the branch, but I clung tight. I held my breath. Aoife stepped inside. *Click, click-a-clack*, went her swan-bill shoes.

"Where is she?" Aoife's church-bell voice echoed 'round the attic. "Where is my daughter? Did you take her?" The footsteps sounded again, quick this time, and the swish of her feather coat ruffled the air.

I inched up another half foot, and my head clanked against the damper. I squeezed shut my eyes, but Aoife took no notice.

Aoife's voice came in a deep bellow this time. "Are you toying with her sweet, helpless little heart, like you did mine, you mangy devil creature?"

There was a whimper, and then a sharp *clap*. Flesh on flesh, Aoife had slapped Darcy.

I bit my lip to keep from gasping. *How dare she!* Anger boiled in my stomach, and I half considered leaping out from the hearth and rushing to Darcy's aid, but that would no doubt only worsen Darcy's situation.

"Thought you'd be treated as a princess?" shrieked

Aoife. "Ha! Coming here and masquerading as my daughter! The nerve."

There was a pound, like a body hitting the floor. I panicked—was it Darcy? But Darcy spoke softly: "I—I didn't mean nothin', ma'am."

And then Aoife said something that made my heart skip. "I bet it was that Lir—that wretched, wicked Lorcan O'Sé—sending over a fake daughter to appease me before he actually *needed* my help. If one thing's for sure, it's that he's not getting her back. And you? You will rot here in the belly of my palace for trying to trick me. You will grow old here, child. You will die here."

Lir? Surely I had misheard.

Aoife's voice lowered, a thin rasp that spilled from her lips like swamp water lapping at a dead tree. "You and I . . . we've something in common."

No, I thought. *Darcy is innocent. She is lovely and pure. You are a monster.*

"We are both prisoners. But only one of us is strong enough to break free. To take what we want without pleading, without kneeling. That is where we differ."

Prisoner, I thought. Had Nuala kept Aoife in America

just as the story said? And then I remembered . . . The story said Aoife would never be granted the joy of love again. Could it be true? *Impossible.*

There was silence, and then the *click-clack* of Aoife's heels. There was a shuffling of boxes or papers as Aoife said, "If I find my child has been here, you're done for."

The yew door slammed shut, and all was quiet. I waited as Aoife's footsteps faded until my muscles could bear it no longer, and then I fell to the grate with a cry of pain. I sucked on my bloody palms until the burning subsided, the bitter taste of ash sticking to my throat. I stood, first rubbing my shoulder from the tension of holding on to the vines, smearing blood all over my sweater—well, technically, Posy-Kate's sweater—and then my hip, which the grate had jammed into when I fell.

Darcy sat frozen on the cot, eyes wide and staring unblinking at a black sack that had appeared in the center of the attic. The stench of rotting meat crinkled my nose as I walked toward Darcy.

"Darcy . . . ," I whispered as I drew close to her. "Why does she keep you here?"

"I . . ." Tears welled in Darcy's eyes. "I skin the swans, Finn. I skin 'em so she won't skin me."

Chapter 29

I TRIED TO KEEP MY VOICE STEADY. *Like a bodhrán drum.* "I'll do it for you."

Darcy and I stared at the sack, fingers pinching our noses to keep the stench at bay.

"Finn," said Darcy, and let out a sigh. I reeled my memory to see if I'd ever heard Darcy sigh before; if there ever was such an incident, it certainly was not like this. Lonely and scared and too grown-up for her own good. The faery god of the winds, long-bearded Borrum, must have manifested in Darcy's breath. "Aoife's lookin' for you. You've got to go."

I shook my head, ash falling from my hair to my tongue like snowflakes. "No way. I en't leavin' you alone with it. I'll make up a story. I'll say I got lost in the basement. Er—does this place have a basement?"

"She'll smell it on you."

I hopped to my feet. "Where's the knife?"

I tiptoe-scurried across the attic and began to rummage in the pile of papers closest to the sack, sifting through mouse-chewed books, old records, bits of postage twine, and other odds and ends. No knife. I pawed through a jumble of headless Barbies and rusty toy trucks. Still, no knife. I lifted the lid of the record player to reveal a stack of envelopes cluttering a dusty Christmas record that looked oddly familiar.

"Finn, *please*." The voice came from just behind me, and I turned to see Darcy staring down at me, red-eyed. "Don't. She'll find out. She knows everything. I—I'm used to it. I've done it thrice before. It—it en't so . . ." But Darcy's face paled with nausea before she could finish. "You've got to be brave, Finn. That's what Nuala would say. You've got to be brave an' let it go, 'cause there's a difference between being rash and being brave," she added for dramatic effect, and despite the stench in our noses, and the soot in our hair, and the bag before our eyes, we burst into giggles.

It occurred to me then that I loved Darcy. That Darcy

filled my heart with joy and hope and lightness. It occurred to me that love is the closest thing to flight I was ever going to get. That wings don't glide on clouds or sunshine, but love. But hope. That before swans learn to fly, they must first jump off bridges and off cliffs. They first must believe that something more beautiful than they can possibly imagine awaits them on the other side. And if they cannot fly, if they fall from the cliff, break their wing on the bridge, bleed on sharp rocks or thorn-bushes . . . if they cannot fly, then they must love. Because love, too, is far more beautiful than they can imagine.

Darcy knelt beside me and ran her fingers along the Christmas record, small bumps trailing under her fingers.

"I play this at night sometimes," she said. "It's pretty and reminds me of Christmastime. Like in Donegal, how the village sets up a tree in the town square, an' Father Cooley makes all us Sunday school kids go caroling, an' I always complain 'bout it, but actually kinda like it, an' how on Christmas Eve Mr. McCann gives out free hot chocolates for the children and Irish coffee for the grown-ups? Yeah. It makes me think o' that."

I leaned closer to read the words 'round the center of the record:

Aoife and Me, Christmas 1945

It appeared to be an exact replica of the record Da used to play me when I was little to hear Ma sing—or at least, Aobh, the woman I believed to be my ma. Except Aobh's copy was called *Aobh and Me, Christmas 1945.*

Sisters, I thought. Just as the story. How strange! Could it be? But, no, stories were just that—stories.

"It's risky," said Darcy. "An' I have to put the papers back precisely how they were early in the morn, because every few days, Aoife comes an' adds another envelope to the pile. But it helps me sleep."

I nodded. "Speaking of risky, I s'pose I should be gettin' on then. I'll come back, though. I promise you that, Darcy Brannon."

"I know you will, Finn."

I half stood, and then slouched back down again as a letter atop the record caught my eye. The return address was from Da's Irish Republican Army office and was addressed to Aoife's manor. The flap was torn open, with a scrap of yellow notepaper stuffed lazily inside. My heart drummed in my chest, down my arm, and through my fingertips. I pulled out the letter and read:

September 28, 1971
Finn,
If you're there . . . if you get this
message, please write to me. I'm
so sorry. Please write. Please
come home.

                    Love,
                    Da

Darcy leaned over my shoulder to read, and we both sat in silence. I placed the letter back onto the record and flicked through the rest of the envelopes, each one opened and each letter crammed carelessly back inside. They were all from Da. My skin prickled, and I remembered a story Nuala told me about a boy who kept such anger inside him that quills sprang from his spine like a porcupine.

That woman—that horrid snake of a woman who dare call herself my mother—was keeping me from him. Aoife was *keeping* him from me. But we would be prisoners no longer, Darcy and I. Oh yes, Aoife was beautiful. Oh yes, Aoife was wicked. Oh yes, Aoife was clever. But she was not clever as I. She knew not how to weave stories out of ash.

Chapter 30

"WHERE HAVE YOU BEEN? I've been looking for you for ages." Aoife's voice was stone cold.

I wrung the water from my hair onto a towel before my bed. Wet soot stained my palms, and I surreptitiously wiped my hands on the underside of my swan-feather blanket.

"I've been here in my room all the time," I said.

"I checked in here, and you most certainly were not here. Why is your hair wet?"

"Er—right. Well, of course I took a shower." That, at least, was true. Aoife would have been even more suspicious if she found me covered in ash. For embellishment, I added, "Haven't washed my hair in days—you didn't notice?"

"Just now? I could have sworn I checked your bathroom as well . . . You know not to leave the table like that. It was most unladylike."

"Right. I just got a bit sad, so I came up here an'—er—hid under the bed . . . Ma," I added for sympathy.

"Hid under the bed? Like a rabid mole rat?"

"Yes, Ma."

Aoife frowned.

"I'm sorry."

These days, my words revolved around loveless "I love yous" and sorrowless "I'm sorrys."

"No matter," said Aoife, striding across the room and settling down beside me on the bed. She laid a skeletal, frigid arm around my shoulder and held me close. Her sweet perfume could not mask the scent of the swan corpse. "*I'm* the one who's sorry, Finbird. How difficult it must be to learn one's father no longer loves them. To have those cherished memories puff up in smoke, like they never meant anything at all. Like they never even happened. I simply cannot imagine the pain of it all."

My teeth clenched and fingers curled. Aoife kissed the top of my head, and I wanted to recoil with the disgust of it, but kept stoic. *I must not let her know.* For Darcy.

"But the thing is, you don't need him. Why should you need your father when you have me? I will always love you, more than the mountains, more than the sun. What matters is that you have me, and I am here for you, always, my Finbird."

My Finbird. I wanted to spit. Nuala used to call me "My Finnuala." Nuala was the only one I belonged to— well, she and Da. I was not "Finbird," and Aoife owned not a toenail, not an eyebrow.

"Now," said Aoife. She stood and grasped my hands, pulling me up as if inviting me to a waltz. Her hands felt like they were made of paper. "Come down for some tea and—"

Aoife's neck tightened, and she glanced down to my hands, eyebrows raised. She dropped my left hand, then flipped over my right and trailed her fingers along the thin red scratches that the thorn vine inside the hearth had made.

"You've been to the border." Her voice trembled. "You tried to climb the thorn trees. You wish to leave me."

"I—not exactly—er . . . They're from my shower comb. The handle had some rough plastic on it." But I doubt I had ever told a lie quite so unconvincing.

Aoife looked up, eyes wide with fear. "How did you escape?"

"I swear—it's nothin' like that—"

But in one motion, Aoife swished out of the room and double-locked the door behind her. From the corridor, I could hear Aoife bark, "Barricade the doors. Bolt the windows. Phone the locksmith," and the squeak of the maid: "Yes, ma'am. As you wish, ma'am."

THE RUMBLING OF FURNITURE being rearranged echoed up the stairs, and two doors slammed as Aoife sentenced her children to their rooms.

"Why should I be punished just because that Finbird did something stupid?" complained Posy-Kate from the hall.

"This is not a punishment, but another word and you'll find out what a real punishment feels like, young lady," warned Aoife.

"Fine," huffed Posy-Kate. "*Obviously*, you love that waterfowl more than me anyway!" And another door banged shut, followed by a muffled "She gets away with everything."

I dragged out my suitcase from below my bed and yanked it open. My orphanage of hawthorn leaves was inside, and I deposited the hawthorn petal from Inis Eala inside for safekeeping, then threw in my Sunday dress. I slammed it shut, pinching my thumb in the latch, sending it shooting for my mouth to suck the pain away. I cursed something nasty as my face tingled and tears burned in my eyes.

I paced back and forth and back and forth until the house went silent, and I slumped against my door. I let the loneliness and the hopelessness creep into my bones, rush through my veins. But then I remembered—the *locket*. I pulled out the half with the photo from my jeans and smiled down at Margaret, Ed, and Oliver.

"Found you," I said.

Margaret gave me one of her probably-too-quick-to-be-real winks, and even Oliver, who normally smiled shyly away from the camera, seemed to tilt his chin slightly my way. And Ed, ridiculous Ed, slyly smirked as always. Margaret laughed. I could hear that laugh in my mind—it was ugly, yes. A bellowing, bumbling laugh with a snort thrown in, like the laugh of a hippopotamus, if hippopotamuses could laugh. But it made me smile.

"I've got to get Darcy out of here," I told Oliver. Then I turned to Margaret, who, in my mind, was the cleverest of the group. "You know any ways out?"

Margaret stared back at me, doll-like. "This is pointless," I muttered, stuffing the locket inside my pocket. I leaned my head against the wall and ticked off all the possible ways to get out. There seemed, to me, only two possible options: doors or windows. Doors, I would have to contact the locksmith for him to make me an extra set of keys. To do that, however, I would have to escape my room to use the phone. But of course, I wouldn't be in this predicament if that were a possibility, now would I?

The other option was windows, but their screens were triple locked, and more recently, four iron bars had been fixed across each window of my room (supposedly to "keep the poor, pathetic birds from banging into the glass"), so it was impossible to break through. But even if I did escape through the window, there would be no way of rescuing Darcy unless I planned on flying up to the roof and sliding down the chimney—

The chimney!

My heart raced. I sprang to my feet and shimmied into my jeans, then threw on one of Posy-Kate's elephant-stitched peasant blouses. If I could just escape my room, I was free. Me and Darcy . . . we'd be *free*. How sweet that word would taste when stirred among the autumn breeze and the oak trees and the cool, soft earth between my toes.

Chapter 31

I CHIPPED A SPLINTER OF WOOD off the bed frame and knelt at the door, picking at the top lock. Luckily, Aoife did not hear the subtle *tick*s and *click*s of the lock, but after what felt like hours of it, someone else did. A *bang* that sounded suspiciously like a shoe whacked at a wall came from Posy-Kate's room, which was to the right of mine.

"Quit it, would you?" The wall between us could not muffle the petulance of Posy-Kate's voice. "That won't work, you know."

I jiggled the lock faster, harder. "Clearly," I muttered, "you've never had something worth breaking free for."

Posy-Kate sighed exceptionally loudly to be sure I would hear it on the other side. "The locks only open from the outside, Finbird. Luckily for you—" There was a *click*, and then Posy-Kate's voice lowered to a whisper seeping in from the other side of the white door: "I'm on the outside."

I dropped the splinter as my door creaked open. Posy-Kate stood there, her outfit having been changed since breakfast. She wore a long white peasant skirt and a chiffon blouse.

"How'd you get out?" I said.

Posy-Kate's voice was a whisper the size of a penny. "Mom doesn't lock *my* door. She's far too preoccupied keeping you locked up to notice me. Besides, even when I do escape the house, she doesn't really care. You're all she talks about. All she's ever talked about." Posy-Kate shrugged, then said matter-of-factly, "Tie your shoes around your neck; we can wear them once we're out, but for now, they'll just squeak. And that top? Ugh! You'll stick out like a lemon tree in a peach orchard. Here—" She shoved a pile of white clothing into my arms. "You'll blend in better. Be quick."

Bewildered, I took the clothes and half closed the

door. I shook open the clothes to reveal a near replica of Posy-Kate's outfit, except my blouse had little birds and fish stitched in blue thread along the collar. I wasn't sure whether to be touched or offended, but either way, I had to stifle a laugh. I changed into the clothes, feeling not nearly as pretty as Posy-Kate looked. Despite my shortness, I always felt lanky and awkward in skirts, but a stark white one simply made my ankles look like chicken legs.

I slipped both halves of my locket into a pocket on the skirt's side and swung open the door. Posy-Kate immediately said, "C'mon." She turned and began to scurry down the marble corridor.

I hurried to catch up, and before she could get far, I tugged on her sleeve. "*What?*" she said.

"Why are you helping me? You hate me."

Posy-Kate rolled her eyes. "I don't *hate* you. You're simply not as refined as Mom and me."

I'll take that as a compliment, thanks very much, I wanted to say, but didn't. Posy-Kate was my ticket out.

Posy-Kate then said quickly and without moving her lips, "Um—sorry. Whatever." She added, "Anyway, if I hadn't let you out, I'd've had to listen to you pick at that lock for who-knows-how-long. Now, Darcy's up on the top floor—I trust you've found her already. I suppose what you lack in looks, your brain seems to make up for. We'll escape from there. Are you coming or not?"

"Coming."

And together, we swept through the swan palace, feathers ruffling in our wake.

WHEN POSY-KATE AND I arrived at Darcy's attic, the swan sack had disappeared, and a smear of dried blood was caked on Darcy's forehead. She gazed up at us, eyes swollen and bloodshot, but then sprang up from her cot and bounced over, nearly toppling Posy-Kate and me over in a hug.

"I knew you'd come," she said, pulling away. "We're escapin', aren't we? How're we escapin'?"

"*Shh*," hushed Posy-Kate. "We must be quiet, Darcy, or Mom will hear."

"Right!" exclaimed Darcy, and then she whispered, "Oops—I mean *right*."

"The chimney," I said. "We're getting out through the chimney. There's a vine in there we can climb—but watch yourself on the thorns."

Crumbs, I thought. We should have brought gloves. We did, however, bring our shoes, so at least our feet would survive the thorns. I hurried over to the chimney, then beckoned for the others to follow. "We haven't a moment to spare. Darcy, you go first. Here—" I pulled her sleeves over her hands. "That way the thorns won't bother you so much. If you fall, I'll be right behind to catch you."

Darcy eyed me warily, but then ducked into the hearth and began to ascend the vine. She squealed with the pain of the thorns, but with a *shh!* from Posy-Kate, she quieted up. I followed suit, bracing myself for the thorns' sting, and Posy-Kate followed behind me. The smoke filled my lungs, and I held my breath to keep from coughing. All was dark, but when Darcy's head bumped against the damper, I said, "Push it up, Darcy. Here, I've got you," and, arms shaking, I held tight to the vine with one hand and used the other to steady Darcy as she slid open the damper.

Sunlight flooded the chimney, and I couldn't help but grin. "Keep going!" I said, letting go of Darcy as she scrambled up the vine with a newfound vitality.

With a squelch of pain, a huge thorn scraped my left

palm. Blood dribbled down my hands, seeping into my blouse and blooming like roses.

"*Quiet!*" snapped Posy-Kate again.

A grunt sounded from above, and then a *clip-clop* of shoes landing on the roof. I looked up; Darcy had made it. She stood victorious on the rooftop, grinning down at us. I strained through the shivers and twitches taking hold of my muscles and focused on her face, even more joy-struck, perhaps, than Ed's.

"*Think of the sunshine, Finn,*" Darcy whispered as I reached for the top of the chimney. "*Think of the breeze.*"

And I did. I thought of the most beautiful scene I could imagine. I thought of the view of Inis Eala from the top of the Slieve League Cliffs. And for the first time since Nuala's death, the memory did not make me feel sad. It made me feel strong. And with one last push, I heaved myself over the edge of the chimney, and clambered onto the roof.

Before I knew what was happening, Darcy squeezed me tight, saying, "You *made* it, Finn. We're free."

Darcy was right. The sunlight felt like magic, and the breeze—I wanted to bottle the breeze and save it for a lonely morning. Bluebirds chirped a sweet melody as cicadas buzzed in harmony, and the *grass*, how wondrous smelled the grass.

Posy-Kate's hand stuck out the top of the chimney, and I turned my attention to her. I grabbed hold of her wrist and pulled. "C'mon," I grunted as Posy-Kate, heavy breathed and sweaty, heaved herself out the chimney.

Her strawberry-blond hair stuck on end and she plucked a thorn from my hair. All three of us exchanged glances—and then laughed in spite of ourselves. Finally, Darcy said, "What now?"

I surveyed the valley. From the top of the manor, I could see all of Starlight Valley—from the little village to the farmhouses, and from the strange and lonely aspen forest to the gurgling ravine encircled by the thick thorn trees. The mountains, the glorious, sun-spotted mountains, cradled Starlight Valley in gentle arms, reminding me dearly of the cliffs of Donegal. And then the tree.

The hawthorn tree Nuala planted when she came to Starlight Valley stood at the edge of a small cliff over the ravine. And there, just beneath its branches, was a black-haired boy and a bird pale as seafoam.

"The tree," I said. "We're going to the hawthorn tree."

Chapter 32

WE DESCENDED AN OLD OAK TREE to get from roof to ground, and once our toes touched soil, we ran, leaving our shoes behind. Barefoot, we scampered under branches, over tree roots, feet kicking up dirt and blowing the fluff off dandelions. We slunk through the village, sticking to the backsides of shops and houses, where rusty pipes clitter-clattered and steam billowed out from kitchen windows.

When the shops thinned and the farmhouses turned to dots in the distance, and at last, the familiar red berries began to squish between our toes, the hawthorn tree slipped into view. Darcy, Posy-Kate, and I climbed the grassy cliff, huffing and puffing and crawling on our thorn-scratched knees as the rushing of the ravine thundered louder and Posy-Kate's complaints grew ever more frequent. ("I've never been so filthy in my life!") And then, as the hawthorn towered over us, a pair of spider-thin legs and hole-speckled boots appeared an inch from my nose.

I stood and smiled at the boy who held in his arms the beautiful swan. The swan's wing was wrapped in an elastic bandage, and her neck draped lazily over the boy's shoulder.

"Sojourn," I said. "What are you doing here?"

"Waitin' for you, of course," he replied, nodding toward the tree for us to follow him. Darcy and Posy-Kate stood, and we followed as he continued, "I said I'd meet you here, an' you said you'd come. At least one of us is good on our word."

"There were . . . complications," I said. Perhaps out of habit, I first felt annoyed, but that quickly ebbed away as I realized Sojourn had waited . . . every day, he had waited for me.

As we ducked under the hawthorn's branches, I slipped the broken locket out of my pocket and set it down against a root, comparing the photograph to the tree before my eyes. The same winding branch stretched out from a gnarled trunk, the same branch that, in the photo, Margaret and Oliver sat atop, and Ed swung single-handed from. The photo looked to me almost identical—except for one thing. In the locket's photo, the thorn trees were nowhere to be seen. The background was simply the view of the valley—sparkling streams and sunlit mountains—and I thought about what Nuala would say if she were here right now.

Imagine how beautiful it would be, she would whisper. *Imagine the view without the thorn trees stranglin' the wild-flowers. Imagine the mountains. Imagine the stories.*

"I know you." Posy-Kate's voice snapped me back to reality. She circled Sojourn as he set Ena down on the carpet of hawthorn berries. "I *know* you." She crinkled her nose at the smell of him—soggy shoes mixed with dead meat. There was not a slightest hint that he had bathed in the past week, no less the past month. "You're that hunter boy. The one Mom gets her swans from."

Sojourn slicked back his oily black hair. "I'm changin' me ways, love."

"How is she?" I asked, bending down to Ena. I dropped my locket onto the berries and stroked her wing. She twitched in pain, and I withdrew my hand.

Posy-Kate scowled up at Sojourn. "I don't like you, boy. I don't like you one bit. And you smell like socks, in case you didn't know."

"Leave him be, Posy-Kate," I said. "He's harmless, if not a touch unpleasant."

Posy-Kate crossed her arms and turned her glare to me.

"What happened to her?" said Darcy, kneeling down to Ena. "And also does she bite? And if so, does it hurt too much to pet her anyway?"

"Fluffy? Nah, she's gentle as a lamb," said Sojourn, kneeling down as well.

"Fluffy?" I gasped. "You named her *Fluffy?*"

Sojourn shrugged. "Have you got a better name?"

"Yes, as a matter of fact, I have."

"Go on, then," dared Sojourn.

"Ena," I replied, tipping up my chin. "Her name is Ena."

The swan lifted her head at that, eyes blazing into mine. Her eyes were like a solar eclipse—dark and bright all at once. Sojourn, for once, was speechless, mouth waggling up and down. At last, he managed, *"You know."*

I narrowed my eyes. "Know what?"

Darcy and I waited with stilled lungs as Sojourn simply glanced from me to the swan and back to me again.

235

Posy-Kate, however, was not as patient. She flourished her hands and burst, "Well, for biscuits and gravy, is anyone going to tell what Finbird's so smart about?" She flopped down beside me, laying her already mud-stained and twig-cluttered skirt delicately around herself so the berries wouldn't further mar it.

Sojourn leaned in close, as if telling a ghost story 'round a campfire. "You know," he whispered, "'bout them Children of Lir." I eyed him suspiciously as he added, "You know you're one of 'em. Admit it, you know."

"It—it's just a story."

"Naw," said Darcy. "Nuh-*uh*. You said it was real, Finn."

I felt my cheeks redden as I stammered, "That was just—that was before, Darcy."

"Before what?" said Darcy. "Before we got proof?"

I shook my head, ash falling to my eyelashes, and breathed, "There is no proof, Darcy."

Darcy crossed her arms and stuck out her bottom lip. "That's the thing about grown-ups—"

"I'm not a *grown-up*—"

"They won't believe nothin', even if it's starin' them in the face." She nodded toward the swan that still gazed directly into my eyes. "They're too afraid of gettin' their hopes up. Like hope's such a heavy thing to carry." Darcy squished a hawthorn berry between her fingers and painted a picture of drippy stars and hearts on her palm. Then, after a minute of silence, she whispered, "But if only they'd pick it up . . . if only they'd heave that hope onto their back, they'd see it only lifts 'em up instead of draggin' 'em down. They'd see hope is made of balloon stuff and bird wings. They'd see."

The swan laid her head in Darcy's lap, and she stroked it with berry-inked hands. I fiddled with the shoe-buckle wing tied to my ankle that Darcy had given me all those weeks ago, then turned warily to Sojourn and said, "It can't be real, Sojourn . . . can it?"

"I knew since the moment I saw you in the forest back in Donegal," said Sojourn. "You're her. You're their youngest sister. An' you know it, love. You've known it all your life."

My heart thrummed against my rib cage. *No*, I thought. *Not possible. No way.* But as Ena gazed up at me with eyes so kind and loving they could have been made of lullabies, my heart whispered, *Yes, possible. Yes, way. Yes, I believe.*

"Hang on," said Posy-Kate. "What even are these Children of Lir? And what's that swan have anything to do with them?"

Sojourn sighed and relayed the tale of the Children of Lir as Posy-Kate, Darcy, Ena, and me sat in silence, listening to Sojourn spin words, with surprising agility, the way a spider spins webs.

"So, you mean to say," said Posy-Kate, when Sojourn finished, "that Finbird is a character from a fairy tale? And that my mother is a faery witch? And that swan is . . . a person?"

Sojourn nodded. "Yep, pretty much."

Posy-Kate's eyebrows rose. "You're *mad.*"

"Mad or not, it's the truth."

"Hang on," I said. "How do you fit into any of this? Why'd you pop into my life that one day back in Ireland an'—an' why're you helping me—er—*are* you even helping me?"

Sojourn's mouth curled into a sly grin, and something Nuala once said about the faery popped into my mind: *"Beautiful, wondrous, wicked creatures. There is nothing inherently good or evil about them, much like their human counterparts. The faery are simply power. What frightens those who do* not understand them is that they appear just as human as you or me. For all I know, you could be a faery, and for all you know, I could be one." And then, it occurred to me that if the story was true, Nuala *was* a faery, after all. She was the half faery that saved the Children of Lir by turning them into swans.

And then I wondered about Sojourn . . . how he flitted about the conversation, how he struck fear and wonderment and power into every word, every movement.

"Because I'm the Children's protector," replied Sojourn. "That's why I—" He eyed Posy-Kate, and she rolled her eyes.

"It's okay," I assured him, and the words felt slippery on my tongue as I added, "You can trust her."

"That's why I work for Aoife," said Sojourn. "That's why I hunt. Anyone else with the job, and those swans would be Aoife's wallpaper. But I save 'em. I make sure Aoife gets her swans, an' I make sure Ena, Fiachra, and Conn en't one of 'em. She only kills the swans to get to the Children, you know. They're the ones she really wants.

"After Aoife exterminated Starlight Valley of all its swans, she started having swans imported from other places to kill, hoping one day three of them would be the

Children. That's what the trains are for. They're magic trains, you see, an' mark my words, you never see the same one twice. They're the only things that've come into this town since Aoife came to reign—the Children and you and me, Finn—and when the trains come, they come filled with swans. Most are dead by the time they get here."

"Wait, back up—what do you mean 'reign'? Aoife's not some queen," I said.

Posy-Kate fluffed her hair and, as if she held some superior knowledge granted only to those clever enough, said, "You don't *know*, Finbird?"

"Why does she call you 'Finbird'?" muttered Sojourn, flicking a piece of dirt from under his fingernail onto Posy-Kate's chin. She wrinkled her nose in disgust. "Stupid name, if you ask me."

I ignored him. "Know what?" I played along with Posy-Kate.

"Mom is the mayor of Starlight Valley," said Posy-Kate. "Practically as powerful as a queen in these parts. No one lives around here, except our little town. I thought that was *completely* obvious."

"Yes," said Sojourn, cutting off Posy-Kate's spotlight. "Aoife delivered all the children in this town. The people hate her . . . but they owe her. They owe her for their children's lives."

"Deliver . . . you mean she's a midwife?"

"Well, a doctor, yes," said Sojourn.

"I was gonna say that," muttered Posy-Kate.

"The only doctor, at that," added Sojourn.

I remembered the faery witch in "The Children of Lir," how she had used her power of life to kill her sister. Was it possible Aoife used the same power to deliver the babies of the valley? To cure people of their ailments?

"No one leaves this town without Aoife opening the thorn trees—she's the only one with the power to control them," continued Sojourn. "But for the most part, she keeps people locked in, an' other people she keeps locked out. She keeps love separated. That's how it's been since she came to this town. Her first day here, she grew the thorn trees, separating mothers and daughters, sisters and brothers, family and friends, even masters and dogs."

I thought of the aspen forest, the notes carved on the white-skinned trees. I remembered the longing and the loneliness and the empty feeling in the pit of my stomach.

"Just like how Lir separated Aoife from her daughter— you, Finn. She can't leave the valley, you know—at least, she can't stray far from it. That was the half faery's curse, remember?"

I nodded vaguely. It all seemed too impossible, too unlikely, too . . . what was the opposite word of seren-dipitous? An unhappy accident? I longed to know. I pulled my broken locket from my pocket and looked from Margaret, to Ed, to Oliver. I wondered if Oliver knew Nuala's secrets. I wondered if she had told him her stories. I wondered if she had told him the story about the very hawthorn tree he leaned against in the photo-graph. The very one my back was curved upon now.

I looked up, and it was then that I noticed a large, sacklike figure bobbing behind a laurel bush in the dis-tance. At first, I wondered if it was not a black bear—but no, black bears did not pick flowers, and this figure was picking flowers. As the figure slipped behind a dogwood tree, words rattled my mind: *unfortunate, luckless, ill-starred.* I shook my head; I was letting my imagination run away from me. Surely, she was simply a villager. If Aoife had sent out security to find us, they would be dragging us back to the manor by now.

"Well . . . well, what should we do?" I said, turning back to Sojourn. "What must we do for Ena? Have you been feeding her properly? What's wrong with her wing? Where do you even live? And if she really is one of *the* swans—and if the others are out there somewhere—how can they be turned back into humans?"

The dark figure tilted its puffy head 'round the dogwood tree. *Jinxed, hapless, ill-fated.*

Sojourn nodded toward the village. "I live in the abandoned mill down the road. I feed her best I can— more 'n *you* can say you've done for her, I might add, and I don't know what's wrong with her wing other than that *something's* wrong and it en't gettin' better.

"And turnin' the swans back human?" Sojourn shrugged. "You've heard it, love. Like says the story: only if she who caused the curse eats the berries from the same hawthorn tree that cursed the swans, will the spell be undone. In other words, Aoife's got to eat berries from that tree on Inis Eala, which is as likely as persuading Posy-Kate to dress as an ogre for Halloween."

Posy-Kate sneered at Sojourn, but even I had to admit, he had a point. We sat in silence until Ena gave a mournful whimper and something suspiciously teardrop-shaped slipped from her eye. *Not possible.* I knew swans. I studied swans. Swans did not cry.

"I still don't understand," I said, turning to Sojourn again. "*You* shot Ena. If you're so keen on protectin' the swans, why'd you shoot her?"

I caught my breath as the figure slipped out from behind the dogwood tree and ambled around the laurel bush, sniffing the pink, star-shaped flowers. *Cursed, hopeless, doomed.*

"If I didn't, the Pegwitch would have," said Sojourn. "I saw her skulkin' 'round the lonely wood and knew she was up to somethin'. If I hadn't shot Ena's wing, the Pegwitch would've shot her heart an' turned her into soup."

"The Pegwitch?" piped Darcy. "Who's the Pegwitch?"

"Oh, she's this batty old woman who lives in a house so wretched she gets her own street name—Pegwitch Way," said Posy-Kate, swatting the air as if surrounded by flies. "Every year at Halloween, some stupid kid tries to toilet paper her front porch, and *every year*, he or she ends up in Mom's living room with vicious scratches and bites. She's a foul one, that Pegwitch. But the funny thing is, she never leaves her house. No one, not even her victims, ever see her. And no one questions her, neither. They're all too scared, I reckon."

Sojourn lowered his eyes to the berry-scattered ground. "Posy-Kate's right—mostly. Aoife's bad, but from what I hear, the Pegwitch is the real monster of this town," he said grimly. "Legend has it, she collects rare families of animals from all over the world. Don't know where she gets 'em all, 'cause the train only brings in swans. And once they're nice and plump, she chops them up into stew. What Posy-Kate en't right about, though, is that no one's ever seen her. Not true. I see her all the time. Usually, she's just a figure, just a shadow, but one day just this summer, I saw her kidnapping the other Children of Lir—Fiachra and Conn, your brothers. There was nothin' I could do. She took them an' she's lookin' for Ena too. An' then, Finn, then she'll come for you."

The rushing of the ravine swelled to a torrential surge—or perhaps the pounding was simply the blood in my ears as my heart *tha-thump-tha-thump-tha-thump*ed. In the corner of my eye, the figure drew nearer. And as it did, I remembered the word now. Nuala had mentioned it once in a story filled with ravens and broken glass and blood-dripping bonnets. The opposite of serendipity was *drochrath*. Oh yes, we four were in for *drochrath* indeed.

"Sojourn . . ." Half by accident, I grabbed his sleeve. "Someone's watching us."

Chapter 33

SOJOURN LEAPT TO HIS FEET. Posy-Kate, Darcy, and I followed suit, hawthorn berries raining down as the tree shuddered. Even Ena wobbled on frail webbed toes. The figure looked up from the laurel bush and tilted its head at us, and Darcy squeezed my hand so hard I began to lose feeling in my fingers.

"*Shh,*" warned Sojourn. His voice fell to a whisper, slow and level: "Finn, listen to me. Run to the village and take a left at the church. Run straight down the hill past five farmhouses and just beyond the fifth one's pumpkin patch, you'll come to the westernmost part of the aspen wood. Run straight through until you reach the gully by the thorn trees. No one goes there. You'll be safe."

"That—that's her, isn't it, Sojourn?" I said, eyes fixed on the figure. "That's *her*."

The Pegwitch lumbered toward the foot of the cliff, hunched back and sacklike patchwork coat coming into clearer view. Her gray-black hair frizzed out from under an overlarge sunhat, and her skin was dark and etched with wrinkles so plentiful her face looked like a topographer's map. A plume of smoke escaped her mouth, and she flicked a cigarette to the ground, stamping it out, before beginning to climb the cliff.

"Yes. But no time for chatter. I'll ward her off as long as possible."

"Sojourn—you have to come with us," I said. "You don't know what she might do to you."

But Sojourn shook his head. "If I do, we'll all be toast— literally. Go, Finn. *Now.*"

"I'm not leaving you here alone—"

"For Darcy," pleaded Sojourn. "For Ena."

Posy-Kate crossed her arms. "What about me?" she whined.

Sojourn rolled his eyes. "And for Little Miss Priss too."

"What's that supposed to mean?" huffed Posy-Kate, but Sojourn had had enough. With a mighty *oof!* Sojourn shoved Posy-Kate and me down the grassy cliff, Darcy and Ena following in our wake.

I stumbled on a tree root and grabbed Darcy's hand the minute I gained my composure, and Posy-Kate heaved up a ruffled Ena. Catching my breath and keeping one eye on the hulking Pegwitch, I turned to Posy-Kate, who bore a thoroughly peeved expression. I nodded toward the village. "Let's go."

I DIDN'T LOOK BACK. We retraced our steps through the village, feet so numb I was positive calluses had begun to form, and once we got there, we slipped down alleyways and clung to the edges of shops, the villagers' chatter whirling to and fro. One conversation, however, caught my ear, and I yanked Darcy and Posy-Kate into a nearby alleyway between MONTGOMERY MAKERS OF FINE VIO-LINS SINCE 1884 and BUMBLEBEE AND BO'S SWEET SHOP. I peeked out and strained my ears to listen. Tidbits of conversations caught my attention. None of it made much sense to me, except for the parts about me, which seemed to be the most popular subject of the day.

"I swear, I saw her, cross my heart," said one woman,

crossing a pair of haircutting scissors over her heart. "Zipped right past my shopwindow as I was cutting ol' Albert's hair."

"Please," said a second woman, "Mayor Aoife'd never let that child out of her sight, no less wander 'round a village unescorted—"

"That's the thing, though—she *wasn't* unescorted. She was with Miss Priscilla-Kathryn. You suppose she finally let them out for a change?"

"I dunno, but if I were you, I'd keep my mouth shut about it. If the mayor finds out you didn't report them when they weren't allowed to be out—or, on the other hand, if you do report them and they *were* allowed to be out—she'll have you tossed out the thorn trees before you can say 'how 'bout a free trim?'"

The hairdresser shrugged. "Wouldn't be so bad. Maybe then I'd find my Marlin."

Marlin, I thought. *That was one of the names etched in the aspen forest.*

A sad sort of silence followed.

"I think about him," said the other woman at last. "Marlin and my little boy. Well," she muttered, fluttering her eyelashes, "it doesn't matter now, does it? That's

249

old talk. As for Mayor Aoife, I s'pose we'll meet the new kid eventually. Rumor has it, Aoife's planning a gala in her honor."

A gala? I surely hadn't heard of such an event. The two women's voices drifted off into the distance, and I turned to Posy-Kate and Darcy. "We can't be seen again. One wrong step, and someone'll turn us in."

Posy-Kate and Darcy both nodded, and we continued slipping through the village, taking extra care to stick to alleyways as much as possible. When at last we came to the backside of a church with tall steeples and intricate stained-glass windows, Posy-Kate collapsed with the weight of Ena. Her face was nearly pale as Ena's, and her arms lay limp in the browning grass.

"This is taking positively forever," she complained.

"Just the farmhouses and the forest to go now," I encouraged, reaching out a hand to pull her up. "I can take Ena the rest of the way, if you'd like."

"It's fine," muttered Posy-Kate.

"You don't look too good, Posy-Kate," tried Darcy.

"I said I'm fine," she snapped, hopping to her feet and heaving a sleepy Ena over her shoulder. "Let's keep going."

So on we went, passing farmhouse after farmhouse, until at last we came to the pumpkin patch, where none other than Sojourn leaned against a rusty blue pickup truck. It was called—according to the chipping letters on the door—ANGELICA, THE BEAUTIFUL, though to me, it appeared anything but beautiful or angelic. The minute Sojourn saw us rise over the hill, he skittered toward us, spider legs flailing.

"Soj—" I started, but he quickly cut me off.

"She's coming," he said dangerously. "She's coming quick—"

Suddenly, Ena let loose a *squawk* and flapped her good wing to fly to safety, but to no avail; she was flightless. She squirmed in Posy-Kate's arms as Posy-Kate stumbled this way and that, face full of feathers. I reached out to catch Posy-Kate as Sojourn lunged for Ena, but it was too late.

"Aargh!" cried Posy-Kate as she tottered backward and smashed into a pumpkin, orange goo spattering everywhere and Ena landing with another squawk beside her.

"Posy-Kate!" cried Darcy, rushing to her side. "Are you all right?"

Posy-Kate's face scrunched, eyes squeezed shut, and her hand shot for her ankle.

"It's going to be okay," I assured her, though my heart was hammering against my chest. I glanced to Sojourn, who looked equally as anxious as me. He bent down and tore a strip of fabric from his sleeve and wrapped it around Posy-Kate's ankle.

"What's that supposed to do?" I said, feeling myself rise to hysterics.

"I saw it in a movie," said Sojourn with a shrug. "Now, c'mon, help me carry her."

"Her ankle's clearly *broken*, not impaled!" I cried, ripping off the bandage as Posy-Kate seethed with pain.

Sojourn's eyebrows knitted, and he fired, "If you've a better idea, then let's have it!"

"'Sides, gee, I dunno, getting her to a doctor? Just *maybe* this whole 'run around town with a so-called magical swan in our arms to escape the so-called swan-eating witch' thing wasn't such a shining idea."

"I'm *trying* to help. An' if you don't believe in the magic, then *fine*! Have it your way, but don't come cryin' to me when that Pegwitch tries to stuff you in an oven or that Aoife turns your precious swan into a pair of earmuffs."

"Stop it! All of you," cried Darcy, stamping her foot in the pumpkin vines. Bits of pumpkin skin and seeds splattered about her feet. "Nanny Hurley said nothin' ever gets done if you don't work together."

"I *can't* work with him," I huffed, grabbing Darcy's hand and dragging her back up the hill. I would simply have to get Aoife; vindictive or not, she was the only one who could help Posy-Kate.

"Well—well you're impossible—*Finbird*! Whatever that means!" shot Sojourn from behind.

Darcy wriggled out of my grasp. "*Finn, stop*," she said, and there was something about her voice—the sheer horror of it—that made me obey. Her eyes widened, and as I followed her gaze, I realized what frightened her so.

The Pegwitch loomed atop the hill.

Chapter 34

SOJOURN AND I QUICKLY LIFTED Posy-Kate and positioned her arms over our shoulders. Ena limped behind us, hurried along by Darcy. "We've got to move. *Now,*" I said.

The Pegwitch trod closer, hand outstretched, and shouted in a voice that sounded like crinkling a paper lunch bag, "Children. Come. I can help you."

"Block your ears, Darcy," said Sojourn. "You're the youngest; you'll be most vulnerable to her spells."

"This is pointless. Just leave me here and save yourselves," cried Posy-Kate, dramatically tossing back her head, perfect waves of strawberry-blond hair swishing into my mouth.

I spat out the hair. "We're *not* leaving you, Posy-Kate." But as the Pegwitch hurried ever forward, surprisingly fast despite her stooped back, my stomach turned with unease. Posy-Kate surely could not run, no less walk. We'd need a miracle, an angel, an . . . *Angelica*.

"Sojourn?" I said, peering around Posy-Kate to look him in the eye. "Do you know how to drive?"

Sojourn snorted. "No."

"Oh," I said. "Well, now's our chance to learn."

"You don't mean . . . you are *brilliant*."

Angelica, the Beautiful, the beaten-down pickup truck, gleamed; rust turned to gold patches before our eyes. The door to the driver's side was permanently bent open, cracks in the windows were taped over with plastic wrap, and the front was splattered with pigeon poo. But the tires were plump and so long as the engine worked, it would do. I peeked in the window—keys were on the front seat.

"I'll drive," I said, dragging Posy-Kate over to the truck.

"But Finn!" squealed Darcy. "The wheel is on the wrong side o' the truck!"

That normally would have made me laugh, but I wasn't quite in the mood at the moment. "Sojourn, you'll sit next to me and pull the brake if things get bad," I said. With a squeal of rusty metal, I yanked open the crooked door as Sojourn heaved Posy-Kate into the passenger seat, his skinny arms quivering and face flushing red.

"I'm not made of bricks, you oaf!" spat Posy-Kate, but for once, Sojourn ignored her.

"Darcy," I said, lifting her by the armpits into the truck, "you'll have to sit on Posy-Kate's lap; this truck's really only meant for two."

Darcy nodded, and I placed a fidgety Ena beside Darcy, then followed Sojourn into the driver's seat. The inside of the truck smelled of spoiled milk and rotting pumpkin. The door barely locked shut as we crammed together, holding our breaths and hunching our shoulders.

"How do we start this thing?" I said, dangling the key in front of me. A myriad of levers and switches, buttons and pedals swirled before my eyes.

"Dunno, but better figure out soon," said Sojourn.

I whipped around to the back window to see that the Pegwitch was but five pumpkins away. *Crumbs.* My heart pounded faster as I frantically began to jab the key in various places, flick switches and pull levers, push buttons, and shuffle my feet. I must have done something right—or, perhaps, terribly, terribly wrong—because then, a great whirring rumbled from below, and the tires kicked up a splatter of mud, and we zoomed into the aspen wood.

Four screams filled the truck as we zigzagged through the trees.

"How do I control this thing?!" I bellowed, flailing my arms around my head as the truck tumbled and swerved on its own accord.

"We're gonna die!" cried Darcy.

"Keep your hands on the wheel, idiot!" Sojourn grabbed the wheel from me, veering us into a thicket of rosebushes, then, decapitating the rosebuds, he added, "I'm pretty sure that's the number one thing they teach you in driving school."

"Well, that's awfully good to know, but *I'm* pretty sure the first thing they teach you is don't run into trees!"

"It wasn't a tree. It was a shrub!"

"Sojourn, LOOK OUT!" I kicked Sojourn in the shin, took the wheel, and swerved away from a thick-bodied sycamore tree in the nick of time. Not a moment later, however, a sparkle of low-lying water came into view among the trees.

Posy-Kate's shriek rattled my eardrum: "Are you stupid? Just stop the car!"

"I don't know how to brake!" Panic rose in my throat, and I slammed my foot against the first pedal I could find.

A great *squawk* let out from Ena.

Darcy pointed toward the gully and shouted, "WE'RE GONNA CRASH!"

The truck screeched, and with a splatter of mud to the windshield, it skidded off a short drop and into the gully below. Water rushed over the hood and leaked into the doors. I covered my eyes, hearing only the crunch of rusty metal and the squelch of tires into mud.

As the water settled and only a gurgle of bubbles remained, I peeked open one eye, then the other.

"Did we die?" croaked Posy-Kate. "We died, didn't we? We're dead."

"We're alive," breathed Darcy. "*We're alive!*"

A ridiculous smile curled my lips, and I repeated, "We're alive."

"For now," muttered Sojourn. "We've got to get you

all back to Aoife before she realizes you're gone."

"Right," I said, though my head was still zinging with *We're alive, we're alive, we're alive!*

I creaked open the door, swampy water streaming down the sides, and with a splash, hopped into the gully. Mosquitoes nipped at my wrists and mud squelched between my toes. "Here, Darcy," I said, reaching into the truck for her. "Sojourn, you carry Posy-Kate."

Sojourn groaned as I pulled Darcy out by the armpits. She clung close to Ena. My knees quivered with their weight, but I managed to carry them, one slimy step at a time, to shore, with Sojourn and Posy-Kate following in my wake.

"There you are," I said, setting her down on the grass and flopping down next to her. I wrung my skirt of the gully water, but the stench—rather like that of a wet dog—could not be masked. Sojourn hobbled onto the grass, dumping Posy-Kate beside Darcy. Posy-Kate puffed with disdain and smoothed out her now completely un-white skirt.

"Does it still hurt?" I said to Posy-Kate. "Your ankle?"

Posy-Kate nodded. "Numbed a bit, but it's simply *agony* every time I try and move it. See?" She flinched her swollen ankle, then grimaced in pain.

"How're we gonna explain to Aoife? We've got to get you to your mom to heal you. Get up, all o' you," I said, hopping to my feet. "Sojourn, you know these woods. You're in charge of gettin' us out."

"Okay," he said, then nodded to Posy-Kate. "But you're dragging *that one.*"

"Don't be ridiculous, Sojourn, I can't carry her myself."

Posy-Kate crossed her arms. "If I'm such a bother, I'll walk on my own, thank you very much." She stood, wobbled on her good leg, and immediately grasped a sycamore tree for balance. The bark chipped under her pink-painted nails.

"Perhaps I can be of assistance?" The voice came from behind, a bouncy voice that played hopscotch between my ears.

I spun around to face a small-boned man, perhaps in his late twenties or early thirties. Though his face was smooth of wrinkles, his hair was flecked gray and his eyes sunk deep into their sockets.

"Aren't y'all a bit young to be ridin' trucks like that?" said the man.

"Clearly," grunted Sojourn as we all turned to see the

truck slowly sinking deeper into the gully, muddy bubbles rising around it.

"Who're you?" I said, inching closer to Darcy to protect her if need be.

The man smiled and held out a calloused hand. "Name's Rodney Bilfer Jr. And that there's my *Angelica*."

My cheeks burned red. "Oh—I—we didn't mean—er—sorry?"

But Rodney flapped his hand. "Don't worry 'bout nothin'. Been meanin' to take her to the dump for ages." He furrowed his brow at Posy-Kate, who held tight to her sycamore tree, and then nodded to her. "What's wrong wi' her?"

"Nothin'," snapped Posy-Kate, shooting me a confusingly dangerous look. "We'll be on our way now." She let go of the sycamore and hopped twice before catching her ankle on a root and wobbling precariously as Sojourn and I sprang to catch her. However, it was Rodney who caught her by the shoulder just before her nose splatted into a pile of soggy leaves—a swirl of reds and oranges.

"All right there, miss?" he said.

Posy-Kate scowled at Rodney, then scowled at Sojourn, then scowled at me.

"*What?*" I whispered. "He's only tryin' to help."

Posy-Kate rolled her eyes, then shooed Rodney off her and leaned in close to me. "He probably works for Aoife," she whispered. "Don't let him fool you—he'll turn us in to Mom, and then we'll really be done for."

"Ah, you got me there," said Rodney, tugging on his large ear. "I do work for Miss Aoife. But let's be honest, who in this town *doesn't* work for her? Don't worry . . . your secret's safe with me." He winked and offered his arm to Posy-Kate to use as a crutch.

Posy-Kate eyed him suspiciously, but reluctantly slung her arm over Rodney's shoulder. "C'mon now," he said. "Young man, come 'round this way an' support Miss Posy-Kate's left side."

Sojourn muttered something nasty, but complied.

"We'll get you back before you're seen, all righty?" said Rodney. With a grunt, he and Sojourn began to carry Posy-Kate through the woods, and me, Darcy, and Ena hurried along behind.

Chapter 35

FOR A SKINNY MAN, Rodney Bilfer Jr. was exceptionally strong. Sojourn, after three minutes of half supporting Posy-Kate on his shoulder, decided he was too completely tired to carry her any longer. So, Rodney lifted Posy-Kate across his arms and carried her himself.

"We're havin' a daughter," Rodney told us, smiling at Posy-Kate. "My wife and me. This is how I'll hold her."

"A daughter?" I said. I looked up to him, and though his mouth was tilted in a smile, his eyes looked tired. Tired, sad, and scared.

"Yes ma'am," said Rodney. "If . . . if she lasts long 'nough."

"What's that s'posed to mean?" snorted Sojourn.

I kicked him in the shin and hissed, "Could you *be* more insensitive?"

"S'all right," said Rodney. "My wife—my Georgie-Mae—she's sick." His voice choked up, and he stopped mid-step before swallowing and continuing on. "Not sure if she'll make it to . . . to when our Lucy's born. That's what we're namin' her. Georgie likes that name. Lucy." He shook his head as if he could rustle away the fears like the aspen trees surrounding us could leaves. "But we gotta keep on hopin', right? All we can do is hope. An' I'm lucky I even have her. Most people, they lost their loved ones after Miss Aoife—all due respect, now—grew the thorn wall. I'm a lucky one, y'know? Yeah."

"You think she'll make it?" Posy-Kate's voice came by surprise—something pretty and small, but, for once, not petulant.

"Well, that's up to Miss Aoife, ain't it?"

Of course. My stomach twisted. "What's she making you do?"

"She hired me to cut down these trees, these aspens with all them scribbles. She wants 'em dead. Don't like the vandalism, she says. But they just grow back. Don't know how, don't know when, but they always grow back."

"So, since they just grow back . . . Aoife won't help your wife or deliver her baby?"

Rodney said nothing, but his face fell ashen, and I remembered serendipity. That was what Rodney needed—a happy mistake. Something like a miracle, but not as improbable. *Something like a miracle, something like a miracle.*

We walked wordlessly out of the aspens, and when we came to Aoife's manor, Rodney left to go tend to the trees again, and Sojourn skittered off with Ena. I had half a mind to send Darcy with him, but at least at Aoife's she was fed regularly and had a stable roof over her head. This was still the best place for her until we could escape the town. Wasn't it? Posy-Kate, Darcy, and I climbed the great oak tree and slipped down the chimney one by one, and when our eyes adjusted to the dim of the attic, we stared in horror.

A pile of ash lay where Darcy's bed had been before.

Tears welled in Darcy's eyes, and Posy-Kate picked up a scrap of paper that lay before the ashes. "She knows," whispered Posy-Kate. "She knows we've been gone." She handed me the paper and I read:

You dare steal my daughter with
your devilish tricks?
Food will be the next to burn.

Chapter 36

POSY-KATE LOCKED ME BACK in my room just in time for
Aoife to come looking for me. She decided to tell Aoife
that she fell down the stairs on her way to delivering
Darcy her lunch. The locks on my door jingled and jan-
gled until, at last, Aoife's swanskin glove appeared in the
doorway, followed by the rest of her, swan-bill heels and
white-feathered cloak.

She was dragging the arm of a little boy about Darcy's
age when she arrived, and when she saw me, she grasped
her heart and said with a sigh, "Oh, thank goodness,
you're safe and sound. I thought I heard noises up here."
She then bent down to the boy, took a piece of gauze, and
wrapped it 'round his forearm, which appeared to have

been cut by glass. "There you are, Timothy," she said. "Off you go now," and the little boy ran off.

"Sorry about that, darling," said Aoife, turning to me. "Too many catastrophes all at once today." When she reached the bed, she sat down beside me and began to stroke my hair. Bits of leaves and twigs fell out from my hair and onto the bed. "My love, my peach, you will be presented."

I was flabbergasted. Clearly, Aoife had known that I had snuck out with Darcy, and all I could blubber out was, "What?" Why was Aoife not angry?

"At your own ball."

So the villagers were *right.*

"We shall hold it on the first of November. Oh, won't it be lovely, my darling? Oh, won't you look pretty? I'm having my seamstress hand-make your dress. You'll simply love it," and Aoife kissed the top of my head.

"Er—okay. Thanks," I said, but through gritted teeth. I knew who that seamstress actually was. I knew what that seamstress would be forced to do to make the dress.

Aoife's eyes sparkled, dark and misty; to my horror, they looked like my own. Aoife clasped her hands together and said, "Excellent. Supper in an hour, all right?"

My mouth felt as if it were coated in sand. "Sure," I muttered, but then something within me remembered, and I tried to keep the panic from my eyes. *I must have left the locket at the hawthorn tree before the Pegwitch chased us!* "Aoife!"

Aoife's eyebrows rose in surprise at the shrillness of my voice.

"Er—um—lemon drops," I decided. "Would you go get me some lemon drops? That would make me ever so happy."

Aoife's mouth did jumping jacks. Then she finally spluttered out, "Sure. I told you that anything you desire is yours. I will have Bruce go to the village—"

"No—er—I want you to get them personally. That would make me the happiest daughter in the world . . . Ma," and for extra effect, I added, "Like mother, like daughter, we know each other's tastes."

"Oh. Of course, my Finbird." There was an excitement—a thrill—in her voice that made me almost pity her. "Of course," she repeated. "But do be ready for your gown fitting when I return," and she let me be, leaving the door unlocked this time.

I waited for the *click-clack* of Aoife's heels to fade completely before slipping out of the room and up to Darcy's attic.

"SHE WANTS ME TO MAKE A DRESS out o' them," said Darcy. "Not sure why. Said she only didn't kill 'em because she didn't want the blood on the feathers."

A cage containing two swans, feathers like white flames, stood in the middle of the attic. The swans huddled together, shivering, with cold or with fear, I did not know.

Anger surged through my veins at Aoife. The idea of making an innocent child murder innocent swans was simply incomprehensible to me. Should I have left Darcy with Sojourn and Ena? "It's gonna be okay," I said. "You're not gonna have to pluck 'em and you're not gonna have to kill 'em—that's a promise," though not one I was so certain I could keep. "Look, I've got to go to the hawthorn tree for a few minutes; I forgot my locket there. But I'll be back in twenty minutes, max. Okay?"

Darcy nodded, and though tears brimmed in her eyes, I had to tear myself away from her.

I climbed out of the chimney just as before, and once I was out, I hurried off in the direction of the hawthorn tree. My bare feet blistered with the twigs and the thorns, but at last, the rushing of the ravine came into earshot, and the familiar squishy berries appeared underfoot. When I caught sight of the silver shining in the sunlight, every muscle in my body relaxed.

I bent down to the twisted root to pick it up—and then my heart leapt into my throat. The locket was fixed. Where Aoife had snapped it in half, it was perfectly melded back together. I picked it up, warm in my fingers, and flicked open the latch. Out fell a tiny piece of a hawthorn leaf with red scribbling on it. I squinted closer and read:

Trust Peg.
—F & C

F and C, I thought, *Fiachra and Conn*. And Peg? The only one I could imagine would be, oh yes, the Pegwitch. I gazed out over the rolling hills to the rickety house at the end of Pegwitch Way, a narrow and winding dirt path lined with overgrown forsythia bushes. I thought about what Sojourn had said about the Pegwitch, but then I considered who I trusted more—Sojourn or the swans, and to be perfectly honest, it was the swans. So I snapped off the necklace Aoife gave me the day I entered Starlight Valley, replaced it with Nuala's locket, and off to the witch I went.

Chapter 37

THE WINDOWS WERE BOARDED, but in the dusk, I could see light seeping out from the cracks in the wood. Smoke billowed from a chimney, and the moon rose, a dusty coin behind the smoke. What was strange, though, were the sounds creeping out the windows and doors, moans and groans, sounds like toppled-over dreams.

I trundled up to the house and was about to knock on the oak wood door when it opened—seemingly of its own accord—and a brown eye peeked out from the crack in the door. Chills scuttled down my spine as the door creaked open. And then a wide, toothy smile came into view.

"*Finnuala O'Dálaigh-Sé,*" spoke the woman, her voice like fire kindling. "After all these years. Come in, child."

My foot trembled on the doorstep, but I took a long breath and stepped into the Pegwitch's house. The sounds grew louder the moment the door closed. It sounded like . . . the willow glades. Birds chirping, squirrels chattering, deer running, fish jumping. It even smelled like the willow glades—fresh water, crisp air, willow leaves in the wind. But it was dark. I could not see a single thing other than the Pegwitch's bushy hair guiding me along a crooked hallway. There was a *click*, a *crack*, a *creak* . . . and then light.

A doorway to what appeared to be a sort of nature sanctuary appeared, a forest within four walls. As I walked inside, tall grass brushed my ankles and a butterfly flitted across my vision. Trees grew tall in the corners and a stream bubbled down the center of the room, a little wooden bridge arched across it. Animals of all sorts hopped and skipped and flapped by—a bunny to the left, a fox to the right, a sparrow up above.

"This is the rehabilitation center for wounded creatures," said the woman. There was a calmness to her voice, despite its crackle, that relaxed every muscle in my body. "You do know who you are, don't you, Finn?"

I wasn't quite sure what the Pegwitch meant, so I

shook my head no, and she whispered, *"The fourth and final Child of Lir."*

"It's true?" Whatever doubt I had felt about the story melted away at just a glance to the Pegwitch's eyes. Perhaps it was a spell, but there was an intense honesty about the wrinkles around her eyes.

The Pegwitch winked, then said, "Only if you believe it to be. Stories depend on belief, you know."

"Oh," I said. "Who are you?"

"I am Margaret Jean Kincaid, but you may call me Peg. Shall we sit?" She gestured to a pair of boulders, and she and I sat on the false-sun-warmed rocks.

"Margaret . . ." I whispered, my hand leaping to my locket.

Peg's face creased into a smile. "Nuala gave you her locket, did she now?"

My voice wavered when I spoke: "How d'you know Nuala?"

"Ah, we were best friends, Nuala and I. Best friends."

"You mean . . . you're the girl in the locket? But . . . Nuala said you were dead."

Peg nodded in that deep way that I knew so well from Nuala. "The hurricane changed everything."

"The hurricane? What hurricane?" I knew I was in for a story, and my bones tingled with the excitement of it.

"We were sixteen, all four of us—Nuala, Ed, Oliver, and me. It started with a squabble between Nuala and Ed and spiraled into a hurricane. Well, when the wind picked up and the rain swept in, Nuala told me and Ed to go fetch our treasures from the hawthorn sprout. That's where we used to hang out, and we'd collect little things from around town—guitar strings, old coins, lost earrings. Small pieces of people. She said she was going to find Oliver, who had run off earlier that day. So, off we went, Ed and me, and what a mistake *that* was. I saw Nuala just before it happened—she stood at the foot of the hill, and then started running toward us. The wind picked up, and we were not strong enough. It blew us right off the edge of the cliff. We fell, but listen now, *we survived*. Oh yes, something saved us—something strange, miraculous, odd, otherworldly—an angel, a faery. Something *magical*. We ended up in the ravine below and took two days climbing our way out. Nuala and everyone believed us dead, and it only took those two days of guilt she felt to send her flying back to Ireland. I never saw her again, but her children, I knew of. She married Oliver, see, and they had two daughters, fair as could be, named Aobh and Aoife. Oh yes. Aoife is Nuala's daughter. Now, I only knew this because I got newsletters from Nuala's little town in Ireland. I tried to send letters to her, but they seemed to get caught in the wind. Well, soon enough, we grew old. Oliver died. Ed died. But me? I'm still here."

"But you don't look like her . . ." I opened up my locket and scooted closer to Peg. Her eyes narrowed as she examined the photograph inside, then said, "That's not me, child. That's your half sister and brothers."

"My *what?*"

"Went missing just this morning. I've been looking for them."

"They're real . . . they're *real*. And so . . . so *I'm* real. I'm the Child in the story." A smile tugged at the edges of my mouth and joy bubbled up in me like Coca-Cola. I felt like a butterfly when it first emerges from its cocoon, the first time it realizes *it has wings*.

"Indeed you are," said Peg. "And I can prove it. That hawthorn tree in your locket's photograph? It was just a sprout when Nuala and I were young. There, it's full grown. Fiachra, Conn, and Ena came to visit it the summer before you were born. I glimpsed them but once, just as they were leaving. That was twelve years ago now. That was the year before . . . before, well, this happened." She gestured to the swans. "But I keep them safe here— at least I did. Aoife captured them not long ago. I would've kept you safe too, but Aoife seems to have gotten a tight grasp on you just under my nose."

"You've got that right," I muttered, and then I smiled down at the swans—my twin brothers. I wondered if they could understand my words.

"When Conn showed up with Darcy on his back, I knew he had made a mistake—she looked nothing like your mother or your father," explained Peg. "But her lungs were badly injured from her near drowning, completely unconscious. She was dying. I knew Aoife would be her only hope; Aoife has a sort of magic touch when it comes to healing people, similar to how I have a certain gift for healing animals. So, I surrendered Darcy to Aoife and told her that Darcy was you—Finn—so she wouldn't hurt her. But then the real you showed up, and all that changed."

"I've got to get Ena to you. She broke her wing— you'll help her, won't you?"

"I will do my best."

"And Aoife . . . we have to stop her before she hurts Darcy—or locks her away forever. We have to stop her from killing the swans, and we have to stop her from separating everyone from their loved ones just because she resents being separated from me. And . . . and I don't love her. I don't feel like her daughter, and I don't want to live with her forever. We've got to do this. You heard she's having a gala for me? You'll come to it, right?"

"I don't know about that. Your mother isn't too fond of me, I'm afraid to say."

"You must come. Please. Aoife has Fiachra and Conn. She must have captured them while they were out writing me their note and fixing my locket. Aoife's got them with Darcy, and Aoife's gonna make Darcy sew a dress out of their feathers for me. That's why she's actually throwing the gala, in celebration of capturing them."

Peg shook her head. "She's quite something, ain't she, Finn?"

"Quite."

"Yes, Finn. We'll stop her. I promise that. In the meantime . . . keep them safe. All three of them—Fiachra, Conn, and little Darcy. Bring me Ena, and I'll take her in."

I nodded. "I'll have my friend Sojourn bring her over. He's been looking after Ena. I've got to get back to Aoife before she realizes I've snuck out."

Peg nodded and took my hand. Hers was warm, soft, and wrinkled; it reminded me of Nuala's. "Well, it's lovely to meet you at last, Finn."

I left after that, trundling back to the manor with a heart that felt as if it had grown wings—tiny ones, perhaps—but wings all the same, beating softly against my rib cage, *thra-thump, thra-thump, thra-thump* . . .

Chapter 38

WHEN I RETURNED, I slipped through the chimney, giving Darcy a sloppy kiss on the cheek, then took a quick shower to clean off the soot. When I came out of my room, I found the mansion to be in chaos. Maids and butlers swarmed the place like bumblebees. They dragged white chairs and tables in and out of the dining hall, brought in marble swan statues and actual stuffed swans, golden chandeliers and diamond-encrusted candlesticks. I stopped one maid in her tracks and said, "Excuse me— er—what is happening?"

"Haven't you heard?" said the maid. "The gala's being pushed up to tonight. I s'pose we'll just have to manage our winter wonderland despite the leaves just turning."

"What? Why?"

"You'd have to ask your mother that, miss." The maid bustled off, and then I gasped as someone grabbed me from behind. *"Darling!"*

Aoife.

"I got your lemon drops just like you asked. Wouldn't believe how difficult they are to find in this little town," she said, dropping a bag of yellow candies into my palms.

"Why is the gala being moved to tonight? Won't people've already made plans?"

"I have a feeling they'll find time enough, my sweet." Her words were like candied apples, poisoned too. "You'll have a marvelous time. We all will," and she embraced me in another hug, then bubbled, "Well, I better be off to the seamstress. Can't have you walking through the doors in these rags."

And Aoife swished off to the foyer. My heart trembled against my ribs. I had to get Darcy, Fiachra, and Conn away from Aoife *now*. Surely, though, Aoife was heading for the attic too. After her clicking went out of earshot, I spun on my heel and hurried for the stairwell.

I scurried up to Posy-Kate's room and banged on her

door. She opened it and scanned me up and down. "You look awful."

"Thanks," I said. "Look, your ma's gonna go make Darcy skin the swans for my dress, but the thing is, these swans . . . they're my siblings. They're Fiachra and Conn. You've got to distract her for me while I get Darcy and the swans."

"But . . ." Posy-Kate tugged at her sleeve. "I just don't know if I can. That's my *mom*. She's all I've ever had. I know it's easy for you, but I can't just betray her like this."

I lowered my head. I couldn't imagine ever betraying Nuala or Da no matter how wrong they were. "I understand."

"I just—I know that what she's doing is terrible, but I just can't comprehend that *she* is the one doing these terrible things."

Posy-Kate heaved a deep sigh and got to her feet, then stumbled out of her room. I gasped as she clutched the doorframe and then I pulled her up by her armpits. "Your ankle—you can't walk."

"It's fine," she said. "I've got to be brave. I know this is right." And then she screamed loud as a banshee's shriek, "MOM! MY ANKLE IS BROKEN. COME FIX IT!" Posy-Kate gave me a smirk and a shrug of her shoulder.

"That should do it, then," I breathed. "Thanks," and I turned on my heel for the attic.

Posy-Kate's cry must have worked, because when I arrived in the vine-twisted attic, I found Darcy and the swans perfectly intact. I clutched my heart the way Nuala used to when I would come home from sneaking out to go climb cliffs on my own.

"Oh, thank goodness, she didn't make you start," I breathed, hurrying over to Darcy. Her eyes were swollen and red, and her lips dry. "We've got to get you out of here," I said, and I turned to the swans' cage, where the two white birds cowered together, necks scrunched to fit the cage.

"I've got the key," said Darcy, and she fumbled through a box under the record player and pulled out a rusted silver key. She skittered over to the swans' cage and chinked the key into the lock, then pulled the door open.

The swans instantly hobbled out, ruffling their feathers.

"Do you think you can carry one?" I asked Darcy.

She nodded, and groaned as she heaved up Fiachra. I did the same with Conn, and we made for the chimney. "Sorry, guys," I muttered as the swans' wings met the thorns, and we began to climb. It was rather more difficult to keep balance on the vines while holding a ginormous swan. The swans squawked and screeched with every brush against a thorn, and blood dripped over my fingers, down my arm. I bit my lip with the swans' pain, but continued to climb until at last that wonderful moonlight blushed into view. I heaved Conn over the edge first and pulled myself up after. Then I leaned over the chimney and grabbed Darcy's hand and yanked her and Fiachra up to the manor roof.

"Where do we go now?" huffed Darcy.

Butterflies fluttered in my chest as if tickling the strings of a harp. "Sojourn," I said. "We go get Sojourn, then we go to Margaret."

Chapter 39

WE FOUND SOJOURN in his abandoned mill, leaning against a stack of hay and feeding Ena a couple blackberries out of his palm. He jumped a bit when we burst open the door, but Ena hardly flinched.

"What're you guys doing here?" said Sojourn, eyebrows cinched.

"C'mon," I said. "We've got to go to the Pegwitch to save the swans."

"The Pegwitch?" spluttered Sojourn, dropping his handful of berries. "But—but—"

"Her name is actually Margaret, and she was Nuala's friend. We can trust her. She's been helping Fiachra and Conn for years apparently. Don't you trust me?"

"Well, you *did* almost get us killed with that truck—"

"*Sojourn.*"

"Whatever, yes," muttered Sojourn, getting to his feet.

"And bring Ena," I said. "Peg might be able to help her wing."

Sojourn nodded and scooped up Ena, then followed Darcy and me out the mill door. We scurried down the hill, past the hawthorn, and up the Pegwitch's winding road. All the while, the sky drifted down, down, down, until a thick layer of fog covered everything down to my ankles. When we reached the oak door, I barely had to tap the door for Peg to swish it open and usher the three of us in.

"There's a storm brewing out there, oh yes, m'dears, I can feel it in my toes," said Peg, the crackle of toe knuckles sounding from Peg's socks-inside-sandals feet. Her dark curly hair was frizzed around her face and her wrinkles more pronounced. She swept through the crooked hallways, patchwork coat fluttering behind her, until she reached the glass door bursting with light. "I see you've found Fiachra and Conn, thank goodness, and dear Ena too," she added, pushing open the door. "And Darcy, sweet Darcy, you haven't a clue of my relief. Come in, come in," and she patted them all inside and sat upon the rock, then beckoned for Sojourn to hand her Ena.

Sojourn eyed Peg skeptically, but with a small grunt, handed over the swan.

"Mmm," muttered Peg as she examined Ena's wing.

Ena squawked as Peg ran her fingers along the gash on her wing. The muddy brown of the half-healed scar made my stomach flop as Peg peeled back the stuck-together feathers. Her touch, however, was so gentle that Ena winced not once as she examined her. When at last Peg looked up, her eyes were grave. "She will never fly again."

My heart dropped into my stomach.

"But she could walk," piped up Peg.

"Walk?" I said. "But—but she's a swan—she has to *fly*." There was simply something wrong about having wings but not being able to use them.

But Peg's eyes simply sparkled. "She could *walk* as human again."

I stumbled back into Sojourn and began to stutter, "What—you mean—you mean—the curse—but how?"

"You know how it goes. If she who caused the curse eats the berry from the same hawthorn tree that turned the Children into swans, the curse will be done. The swans will be free."

"So Aoife has to eat a berry from the hawthorn on Inis Eala?"

"Unless I am mistaken, yes," said Peg.

"So how do we get a berry before the gala? It's practically impossible," said Darcy.

Peg's dark eye twinkled and she repeated, "Practically."

Something tickled my foot, and I was suddenly aware of the tiny piece of metal strapped around my ankle: Darcy's shoe-buckle wing. And then I thought of what Nuala would say, and it probably would be something like, *Miracles are made of wings you forgot were on your back.* But the funny thing was, my miracle didn't seem so big anymore. It wasn't a huge mountain to climb. I still wasn't complete without my family. I would never be until we were reunited in full. But I had my friends. I had Darcy and Posy-Kate, and even spider-legged Sojourn. And I had the swans. I loved them. I remembered the deep emptiness, the loneliness I had felt under the hawthorn at Inis Eala. That tree stuck in my mind, branches like Nuala's wrinkles, like Peg's, like the ones on my palms that would spread with more stories. I was going to make more stories.

I turned to Sojourn and started, "We've got to get to the—"

"So, it's you." The voice slipped through the air like skates on ice.

I spun around to face Aoife towering in the doorframe. Her lip curled as she sneered, "Those swans will be slaughtered, naked, before all my people. You" —she turned to me, forced smile cracking her lips— "will wear their coats."

"*No*," I screamed, my voice breaking as I lunged in front of Ena.

"You're not taking the swans anywhere," said Sojourn, clenching his fists.

Aoife trilled with laughter. "Watch me." She took three click-clacking, swan-bill-heeled steps forward and bent down before me so I could smell the hunger on her breath.

"Come, Finbird. Or watch your little friends die."

I felt my blood drain from my head down to my toes with the intense fear of unknowing just how far this woman would go to get what she wanted.

Aoife stood and yanked Darcy and me by the wrists. "It is time for the gala. And you two—Margaret and my hunter boy—don't you think for one minute you will not soon come to face your punishment."

And so Aoife swept Darcy and me outside, fingers like thorns digging into Darcy's scalp, forcing me to follow suit.

Chapter 40

THE FOG HAD BEEN REPLACED with a bitter chill. The grass snapped with frost as Darcy, Aoife, and I scurried up the hill to the manor. Aoife held Ena by the wing as she screeched in pain. Aoife had told Peg that a servant would return for the other two swans, and if she tried to hide them, Ena would die immediately. The light from the lanterns around the manor glinted off the windows, and a path of white feathers had been laid on the ground.

"No need to worry, dear," said Aoife, turning to me. "Everyone is here to celebrate you, to welcome you officially to Starlight Valley. Don't be glum, Finbird. Let me see you smile."

I forced a grin onto my lips as we walked through the

front doors, though my mind was abuzz with fury. Music blasted from the dining hall, a harmony of violins and cellos and pianos, the sort of music Nuala called fancy-schmancy. The chandeliers were lit, and a distant chitter-chatter could be heard from the dining hall.

"Go to Posy-Kate's room, Finbird. She will watch over you while I have your dress fixed. Go on, now," and Aoife shuffled me up the stairwell.

I did as I was told, but my mind raced with thoughts of how I could save the swans and Darcy. How was I supposed to get a berry from the hawthorn tree in Ireland? That was over three thousand miles away. I would need a miracle. I would need serendipity. And I knew exactly what we had to do.

I barely had to knock on Posy-Kate's door before she pulled it open and yanked me inside. A white bandage was strapped around her ankle, and a pair of crutches stood against her bedpost.

"So what're we gonna do?" she asked immediately, hurrying me over to her bed.

"We've got to go to the hawthorn tree," I whispered.

"What?" said Posy-Kate.

I looked up at her blazing blue eyes. "The hawthorn," I repeated. It was far-fetched, but it was all I had to go on. "That's where I've got to go. Sorry, would take you with me, but you can't walk."

Posy-Kate put her hands on her hips in protest, but I gave her a quick hug and said, "Don't worry. I'll be fine."

Her collarbones tensed, but she nodded and let me go.

The paranoia of Aoife finding me prickled the hairs on my arms as I crept out into the hall. She would be in the attic with Darcy, that was for sure. I could simply go out the front door as guests arrived, no problem, I thought, though really, I wasn't sure if it would be a problem or not. Surely a maid or cook would see me. It was then that I realized the difference between being brave and being rash. Being brave helps people. Being rash doesn't help a soul. Now was the time to be brave. I needed a disguise. So, I rushed for the laundry room.

"Oh—Miss Finnuala," exclaimed three maids in surprise when I rushed into the laundry room. One dropped her laundry basket and knelt down to gather the contents, her face blushing scarlet. "What—what can we get for you, miss?" she asked.

"Oh, noth—actually . . . I need some undergarments for my dress. It doesn't have as much pouf as I need it to."

The maids clasped their hands together, and yes

indeed, I walked out of the laundry room with three baskets full of maids' skirts.

Once dressed in the maid's uniform, down the stair-well I went. I zoomed for the front door. The gold door-knob was in my reach—just when whose slinkety voice did I hear, but Aoife's. My heartbeat raced as my eyes darted to find a cover-up. Maids, butlers, and chefs zig-zagged in front of me. I jumped up and grabbed a hat off one of the chefs to cover my white-blond hair and rushed over to the sweets table. I ducked underneath and waited for Aoife to pass by, not to mention the confused chef whose hat I'd just stolen. When all was clear and Aoife's voice faded into the distance, I crept out from under the table, then out the front door, then into a swirl of dusty, billowing snow.

THE HAWTHORN BERRIES were droplets of blood in the cotton-soft snow. I followed their trail, wind whipping my face, up the red-and-white hill to the crooked tree hanging off the edge of the cliff. One lanky and one baglike figure each stood silhouetted in the mist at the top, and as I stumbled closer, I realized I knew them.

"Sojourn—what're you doing here? Peg?" I was panting, hard.

"Waitin' for you of course," said Sojourn. "This *is* kind of our place, is it not? Can you believe it's snowing in *October*?"

I hadn't time for talk about the weather. "This hawthorn," I said, running my hand along its trunk, "it's grown from a seed of the one on Inis Eala. Nuala told me she planted it when she immigrated to America. The story goes, before she left Donegal, she took a seed from that tree, and kept it safe until she got to Starlight Valley. She planted it to make her feel more at home here, to have a little piece of Ireland with her. So this hawthorn, he is the child of the hawthorn on Inis Eala. These berries hold the magic capable of breaking the curse!" *And that*, I thought, *is* my *story*.

"Clever girl," muttered Peg.

"Do you think it matters how ripe it is?" I said.

Sojourn shrugged. "I dunno. How would *I* know?"

"Never mind, we'll gather a few, just in case," and I frantically plucked some berries from the tree, then pocketed them into my jeans. "Now all we've got to do is get Aoife to eat one. I think I just might have an idea of how. C'mon. Let's go back to the manor."

Chapter 41

SOJOURN, PEG, AND I slipped into the house among all the other guests arriving for the gala. *My* gala. We went one by one up the grand stairwell in a long process of leaving for the bathroom and returning from the bathroom in variations so as to not look suspicious, and slunk into Posy-Kate's room.

"You're here," she said, spinning around from her bed. She spread her arms across her bed—that looked oddly disheveled—as if hiding something, then said, "I have something for you, Finn." She scooted to the side to reveal a long and flowing dress, white and sewn of feathers and strips of cotton and lace. Scraps of comforter and curtain lay behind the dress. "Fastest I've ever sewn something in all my life. Just hope it fools her—and that it doesn't fall apart."

"It—it's perfect. Now Darcy won't have to skin the swans, once Aoife gets a look at this—she'll think Darcy made the dress. Go give it to Darcy so she can give it to Aoife."

Posy-Kate nodded and hobbled away.

Not an hour later, there was a knock on the door, and Posy-Kate's voice rattled a little too excitedly, "Dear sister Finn, Mom has your dress for you here!"

Peg and Sojourn hid behind the door as I opened it. I was greeted by Posy-Kate and Aoife. Posy-Kate stepped inside, and Aoife smothered me in a big hug. "Beautiful, isn't it darling?" she said.

I nodded. "Exquisite." That was a word I learned from a storybook long ago. "I'd like it to be a surprise—you seeing me in it. May I have some privacy?"

"Of course," and she kissed me on the forehead, lips dry and cold.

Peg and Sojourn turned as Posy-Kate helped me into the dress. It fell perfectly to my ankles, fitting me like a snow angel would my every inch.

"How do I look?" I said, tentatively turning to the mirror on Posy-Kate's door as Peg and Sojourn turned around.

Sojourn crossed his arms and eyed me up and down. "Like a Finbird. Whatever that is."

I rolled my eyes, then said, "Let's find Darcy. We've got to move fast so Aoife thinks I'm still getting dressed. C'mon, we haven't time to spare."

AND SO THE FOUR OF US scurried up to the attic and told Darcy of the dress and the berries.

"I want to help," she said. The vines overhead were thicker than usual, the thorns sharper. Fiachra and Conn, and now Ena were back in their cage.

"No," I said. "I've got to do this on my own. Besides, I need you four to keep the swans safe."

"You don't have to do everything on your—"

"I'm not arguing about this, Darcy. Keep the swans safe. I'll be fine," and I kissed the top of her head, cinders collecting on my lips. I turned to Sojourn, Posy-Kate, and Peg, whose eyebrows were all furrowed, and I repeated, "I'll be fine. Okay?"

They nodded, and I took a breath, then turned for the door.

AOIFE'S KITCHENS WERE A DANK PLACE, low ceilinged and swirling with steam. Dishes clattered and servers carrying trays of miniature foods weaved in and out of the maze of counters. A few cooks glanced my way, but none asked questions. It smelled of roast beef, cabbage, fresh whipped cream, and sweet wine. I caught a whiff of cherry pie and followed the smell to a small silver platter set on a corner counter. The platter held a dozen bite-size cherry pies, each one crisscrossed with steaming crust.

I uncurled my handful of berries and slipped one into one of the pies, then scooped the pie into my hand and hid it behind my back as I skittered out of the kitchen and into the dining hall.

The room swelled around me, lights bursting like kaleidoscopes in my vision. The chatter stilled as all eyes turned to me. Aoife bustled through the crowd to the doorway where I stood. Her eyes were bright, but I could see the irritation creeping behind them. She held up a smile on her face like a puppeteer would a marionette.

Her voice was breathy and startled when she spoke. "May—may I present my daughter, Finnuala Rose O'Dálaigh."

The hall burst with cheers and my eardrums wobbled in my ears. Aoife calmed the crowd and she began to speak again, a thrilling speech for sure, but my ears seemed too muffled to be able to hear. Everything felt larger than normal, then smaller, then larger again, as if I were Alice in Wonderland, growing and shrinking and toppling and turning. At last, Aoife raised a glass of champagne and proclaimed, "To Finnuala!"

The crowd chanted in reply, "To Finnuala!" and then the music played and everyone went back about their business of dancing and munching and chattering.

I turned to Aoife, joints shifting like rusted wheels. She fake-smiled down at me. "Why, isn't this splendid, Finbird?"

I nodded vaguely and then slowly revealed the cherry pie. "I—I made this for you. To thank you for—er—all the wonderful memories we've shared. And all."

"Oh?" Aoife gazed down to the pie for what felt like an hour, then, with dainty fingers, she took it and bit into it. "Mmm," she said, crumbs scuttling down her shiny white suit. "Very nice, Finbird. Delicious." And she finished off the pie, licking her fingers.

I stared at her, waiting for something to happen. Nothing changed. Not even a twitch. Eventually, Aoife raised her arms. "Well," she said. "Go on now, enjoy the party. It's all for you."

"Right—er—thanks. Thank you."

Chapter 42

"IT SHOULD HAVE WORKED." After talking to a few curious guests, I had slipped out of the party momentarily to "freshen up," and climbed back to the attic to find Peg, Posy-Kate, Sojourn, and Darcy around the swans, who had been let out of their cage. "She just stood there. Nothing happened," I said. "And they're clearly still swans too."

"Peculiar," said Peg.

"She who caused the curse must eat the berry. Maybe we really need it from the real tree back in Ireland."

"If that's so, we're doomed," muttered Sojourn.

"Well, we've got to do something soon," said Darcy. "It's half past eleven. Aoife's gonna kill the swans at midnight, like a fireworks show or something. She thinks I kept 'em half alive just so she could kill them later."

"I know," I said.

"Finn?" piped up Darcy.

"Mmm?"

She took my palm and let the leftover berries fall into her hands. "I forget. Why did Aoife want to kill the Children of Lir in the first place anyway? I mean, they were just children. What did they ever do to her?"

"Because the older children took away Aoife's baby. She was just a mother, just a mother who had been over-shadowed by her sister all her years growing up, and at one time just an innocent child. She was born . . . innocent. Darcy—you're a genius."

"What? What'd I do?"

"Everyone acts for a reason. Aoife, she may have cursed the berries in the first place, but she didn't cause the curse—*I* did. When I was a baby. I was what Aoife and the Children were fighting over. The Children ate the berries to save *me*. You know what this means?"

Peg's jaw grew tense. "A-are you sure?"

Darcy looked from Peg to me, then back to Peg. "What's she sure 'bout?"

"Finn—you don't have to—" started Posy-Kate.

"Yes, I do. It's the only way. I have to eat the berry. It's the only way to free the swans and to free you, Darcy. And to free myself."

Peg spluttered, "But you haven't a clue what will happen if you—"

"I'll just have to test my wings."

Just then, footsteps echoed from outside the door.

"No," whispered Sojourn.

"Hide," I said, and everyone shot to their feet and began to search for a hiding space. "Up the chimney—all of us can fit if we squish. You go first, Darcy, then Posy-Kate, then Sojourn, then Peg, then me. C'mon," and I hurried over to the fireplace. I lifted Darcy up the chimney and she caught hold of one of the vines and climbed her way up. Next, Posy-Kate limped into the fireplace and heaved herself up into the chimney. Then Sojourn, long-limbed, spider-slunk his way up. Peg was a bit large for the chimney, but she sucked in a breath and squeezed up too. I stepped into the fireplace—

A brush of clothing against the half-open door. The door swished open. And there stood Aoife. Her face was ceramic as a statue as she stared at me. And then she broke her stony gaze and yanked a handful of feathers off my dress. "Fake." She shook her head and nodded to the chimney. "So this is how you've been sneaking out," she breathed, and then she puffed out her chest and spat, "Ungrateful brat. I give you everything you could possibly want, and this is how you repay me? You should be ashamed."

I bit my lip, but said nothing.

"For the rest of the night, you shall stay here. That chimney will be nothing but thorns."

A cry of pain let out from the chimney, and Peg, Sojourn, and Posy-Kate fell out, arms and legs covered in fresh cuts. Darcy must have gotten out. New vines tumbled out of the chimney at Aoife's will, thorns thicker, sharper, than any I had seen before.

"I knew you were smuggling in street scum," said Aoife to Darcy when she saw Peg and Sojourn. She huffed and tilted up her chin. "And you," she said to Posy-Kate. "I can hardly call you my daughter anymore. I raised you, Priscilla-Kathryn; I made you everything that you are. I suppose it *is* true what they say about adopted children."

Posy-Kate clenched her jaw, and I saw a tear creep out the edge of her eye.

Turning to me, Aoife said, "I only do this because I love you." And then her gaze turned to the swans. She collected them, returned them to their cage, and heaved up the cage. "We'll be on our way," said Aoife, and she swished out of the attic.

Peg turned to me, face dripping with blood. I tore off the sleeve of my dress and dabbed at the wound. "Eat the berry," she said. "Eat it now."

My palms fumbled for a moment before something hard dropped into the pit of my stomach. "Darcy—she has the berries."

Chapter 43

"THERE'S GOT TO BE A WAY OUT of here," I said.

"Face it, Finn," said Sojourn, "we're done for."

"No," I said, grinning. "We're not. And you know why?"

Sojourn and Peg both looked skeptically to me. "Because," I said, "I'm *her* daughter. I'm Aoife's daughter. Which means she's not the only one who's part faery. She's not the only beautiful, wicked, wondrous creature here. Nuala always said that for all I know, I could be a faery, and you know what? All I've got to do is find the faery in myself too."

I approached the chimney, swan feathers trailing in my wake, and stood before the mass of thorns. Snow filtered in from the top, and as I enclosed a vine in my hands, the chill of it sent a shiver down my arms. I closed my eyes and wasn't sure what to think of, so I let the cold in and let the warmth out of my fingers. I imagined the sun on my back the first time I escaped the manor, and I imagined the warmth of Nuala's hands around my own. I thought of Darcy's smile. I thought of all the stories I had no reason to believe in, but I *believed* in them. I believed in the swans, and I believed in the faery, and I believed in Darcy, and most of all, I believed in myself. And then I gave my belief a pair of wings. I believed in the serendipity of flightless things taking flight, wings spread wide, flying away.

Peg's voice drifted in from the back of my mind. "Well, I'll be."

Sojourn ran his fingers through his hair and whispered to himself, "Holy flutherin' faeries."

I peeked open my eyes. Before me, the tangle of thorns had been replaced with periwinkle flowers, petals velvety soft. I smiled, then laughed in spite of myself. "That's it," I breathed. "That's it, we're free! Come on!" and up the chimney we crawled.

We found Darcy on the roof, eyes wide. "Did you see that?" she bubbled when we tumbled out to her feet.

"Did you *see* those flowers just appear?"

"Yes, Darcy," I said. "Now, you have the berries?"

Darcy nodded and handed over the pile of berries.

"I may've dropped a few."

"It's okay," I said. "If all goes as planned, I'll only need one."

My heart thrummed against my chest, steady but heavy, like it had grown swan wings. Snow caught on my eyelashes, and fog blurred my vision. The greyman's mouth opened wide, and I let it envelop me as, fingers trembling, I lifted the hawthorn berry to my lips and swallowed. It tasted bitter, but the taste left over in my throat was sweet, like brambleberry pie or Mr. McCann's warm apple cider. I opened my eyes, realizing only then that I had closed them. I looked down. My shoes were still there. I was still me. My heart was still beating.

"The dining hall," I said. "Let's see if this berry worked any magic."

We climbed down the oak tree, scraped knees and bruised elbows, then flung open the front doors. Shrieks met our ears as we hurried inside. When we reached the dining hall, we were met with a scene of disarray. Tables were toppled over, silverware was splattered across the floor, and chandeliers hung at odd angles. A man in the corner stomped out a flame from a curtain and a woman pulled a child from out behind a flipped chair. And above it all circled a single swan, wings spread wide, but toppling through the air as if it had never flown before, with people gazing awestruck at it. Fiachra, Conn, and Ena, however, were nowhere to be seen. Nothing but an empty cage lay in their place at the head of the dining hall.

I turned to Peg. "You don't think . . ."

"Indeed I do."

"*Aoife*," I breathed, smiling up at the swan. "We did it. We reversed the curse. But then—where are my siblings?"

A low rumble sounded from outside, almost as if a thunderstorm were rolling in. But then came a whistle. Thoughts whipped through my mind lightning fast, and I turned for the foyer. Footsteps followed in my wake, but I hadn't the time to see whose they were. I burst open the doors, and indeed, just before the manor lay a line of thin silver train tracks. The sound of an engine chugged louder as a navy-blue train grew larger in my vision until, at last, the wind smacked my face and the whistle blared in my ears, and then . . . silence.

Smoke danced with the snow. In the distance, the

swan—my *mother*—flapped about at the edge of Starlight Valley, and I could see the thorn trees begin to wither like the chimney vines had, as if on demand. Sighs of wonder and relief encircled me. I turned my attention to the train again, and as the passenger doors opened, out stepped three young adults, two men and one woman. They were tall, hair pale as seafoam, eyes dark as midnight, and lips red as hawthorn berries. They emerged from the smoke, and the woman smiled in my direction.

"We're looking for our sister," she said. "They call her Finnuala."

Epilogue

EACH ONE OF US was a tiny sunflower seed, rough to the touch and cloaked in black, drifting through the ragged wind. Not a hat nor a hair out of place, we were black swans, flocking to the final resting place of our beloved storyteller. Father Cooley said the prayers, and we sang "The Parting Glass," no one looking at another, but all gazing out to the mainland. Though the sky grayed and the grass across the isle turned to mist and the clouds rumbled with ominous thunder, the water was still. It seemed that today Inis Eala mirrored Nuala's soul.

As I cradled Nuala in my palms the very way I did Rodney and Georgie-Mae's new baby girl, Lucy, I remembered the Virginia mountains. I wanted to climb them when I went back. I wanted to meet the people. I wanted to feel that hot American sun on my neck.

Just as the thought drifted into my mind, I felt a warmth against my shoulders, the calloused hands I knew to be Da's. Conn and Fiachra stood on either side of Da. Beside me came Darcy, hands held by Sojourn and Posy-Kate, and then Ena on my other side, leaning down and kissing my cheek. It felt like a story, that kiss.

I tiptoed to the edge of the cliff where the hawthorn tree stood nearly bare and shivering. My naked feet crunched frost underneath me as I came to the very edge, toes curled over the ledge. A tear snuck out the corner of my eye. But when I thought about it real hard, it wasn't such a long way to fall.

As my fingers creaked like old doors and rickety stairs, I closed my eyes and whispered to Nuala, "Your family is home, Nuala. Me and Ena and Conn and Fiachra too—we all came home. You were the sort of thing miracles are made of. I promise I'll make miracles too."

I opened my palm. The ashes slid through my fingers and drifted into the November wind, slipping away like the heather I used to dream about. That *other* place I used to dream about. I wiped that tear away.

After all, it wasn't such a long way to fly.

Acknowledgments

Without the help of many people, this book would not be a book. I want to thank the entire team at Yellow Jacket and New Leaf Literary & Media for their work, kindness, and patience, as well as my family and friends for their support. At Yellow Jacket, thank you to my editor, Charlie Ilgunas, and the publisher, Sonali Fry. Thank you to the editorial assistant, Courtney Fahy; the copyeditor, Anne Heausler; and the managing editor, Dave Barrett. Thank you to the designers, Rob Wall and Natalie Padberg Bartoo; the publicist, Paul Crichton; and the marketing manager, Nadia Almahdi. At New Leaf Literary & Media, thank you to my agent, Suzie Townsend, and her assistant, Cassandra Baim. Thank you as well to Jaida Temperly, who helped me begin my career. Thank you to Con Moriarty for guiding me through Ireland. Thank you to my family, friends, and mentors. And most of all, thank you to my readers for your support and beautiful imaginations.